"That's what I'm s

I don't know why I chose to call Noelle. Well, that's not true. She and I had some kind of weird connection when it came to guys. I think she saw me as "safe" with her secrets because of our age difference. And she'd told me a few. I guess I trusted her, as well.

I'd stretched out on the sofa, wrapped up in a velvety blanket. A vanilla candle emitted a soothing fragrance. I watched as the flame danced. My roommate had left town and wouldn't be back until after Thanksgiving—some people actually liked the holidays instead of dreading them. I was glad she was gone so I could be lazy. Her OCD-ness kept me perpetually on my toes. Today I only wanted to figure out the conflict happening in my brain.

"You can't be kissing your therapist, Chrissy. You can't be kissing your therapist." She used her big-sister-knows-best voice.

"Eww, yuck. I didn't kiss my therapist. I said I met him at the therapist's office. They're very different things."

She let out a breath. "So you didn't kiss Dr. Peterson?"

"Oh my gosh, Elle. Are you even listening to me? Why would I kiss Dr. Peterson? He's old. I think I'm going to be sick."

"Sorry. Okay, so you met some guy at the clinic and kissed him in the snow."

Now *I* let out the frustrated breath. "Close enough."

The Christmas Frost Series

FINDING JOY
NOELLE'S KISS
HOLLY'S HEART
CHRISSY'S CATCH

These are the stories of the four Frost sisters, who overcome heartache, betrayal, and ghosts from the past to find true love and bring back the magic of Christmas.

Chrissy's Catch

by

Jeanie R. Davis

Christmas Frost, Book 4

Chrissy's Catch

Cover Art by *Kim Mendoza*

The Wild Rose Press, Inc.
PO Box 708
Adams Basin, NY 14410-0708
Visit us at www.thewildrosepress.com

Publishing History
First Sweetheart Rose Edition, 2019
Print ISBN 978-1-5092-2925-3
Digital ISBN 978-1-5092-2926-0

Christmas Frost, Book 4
Published in the United States of America

Dedication

To Avonell Rappleye, my wonderful mother,
who inspired my love for writing

Chapter One

Gasping for air, I clutched the countertop while everything spun out of control. "I can't breathe. I'm going to die." My chest constricted, and my heart pounded, echoing in my ears.

"Chrissy, what's going on?" My sister's voice on speakerphone snapped me from the attack. I gulped air like a parched camel guzzling water. Of all people to have heard me freak out, it had to be my over-protective sister Elle.

I hadn't had an anxiety attack in months. I looked around for a trigger. Aha! My eyes landed on a new note from my roommate. She rarely left notes, her messages generally came in texts. Her handwriting, so eerily close to my late mother's, must have set me off. Elle couldn't find out—she'd have me committed.

"Chrissy. I'm coming over there."

"No. I mean, sorry, Elle." I infused my voice with cheery optimism and forced a laugh. "I saw the cutest guy walk past my window. Uh…he took my breath away. Thought I might die." I rolled my eyes at my corniness.

"Now I know something's up. Since when do you get all gaga over a guy?"

Noelle was right. Years had passed since I'd opened my heart to a man. I'd had casual flirtations, but nothing serious. What had happened? Did I not trust

1

them? Or was it me I didn't trust?

"Chrissy?"

"I—I guess you had to be there. Anyway, I'm fine. What were you saying?"

Dashing to the bathroom, I splashed water on my face, closed my eyes, and took three long breaths. *You've got this, Chrissy*, I told myself, shrugging off the attack. My pale reflection in the mirror said otherwise.

"I asked how you're doing," she said.

I needed comfort food. Chocolate. A secret stash in my bedroom called to me. I grabbed a bag of M&Ms and made my way to the living room where I flopped onto the sofa, juggling the candy and a water bottle. Noelle tended to be chatty. I might as well get comfortable. She wasn't my oldest sister, but definitely checked up on me the most. All three of my older sisters smothered—I mean mothered—me.

I took a deep breath, feeling much better now. "In other words, you want to know if I went to my appointment with Dr. Peterson today?"

Noelle laughed as if I had completely missed the mark. Silence. "Okay, yeah. Did you go?"

"I knew it. And, no. I didn't go—"

"Chrissy—"

"Because his receptionist rescheduled me for tomorrow. Wow, Elle. Give me some credit."

"Sorry. You've been doing so well. I don't want you to…" She paused, probably because she couldn't think of a graceful way of saying she didn't want me to take another nosedive into that dark abyss I'd lived in for the first two years after our parents died. A Christmastime car accident had claimed their lives, and

I'd struggled through the holidays ever since. No way would I tell her about the little episode I'd just had. The attack had been minor, after all.

"I know, Elle. I don't want that, either. And I'm doing great." I took my voice up a notch to a happier pitch. "My marketing job's good; I live in the most beautiful green spot on earth—surrounded by mountains, hills, and trees; I like my roommate, Kassandra—who wouldn't? She's hardly ever around, and when she is, she likes to clean; and I've got three awesome sisters." I paused. "Should I go on?"

"Are you dating anyone?" She knew I hated that question.

"Nope, but you'll be the first to know when I am." I knew she hated that answer.

"You don't have to get snarky about it. I'm interested, that's all."

"I know. But, Elle, we see each other almost every week. I think you'll know when there's someone I'm interested in. What about you? Are you dating anyone?"

Noelle had been through a brutal divorce. She deserved a great, noncheating man to sweep her off her feet. Her ex was one of the reasons I'd sworn off men. Who needed that sort of pain?

"Touché, little sister. Did you hear the news?"

"What's that?" I opened the water bottle and took a sip.

"Richard Arnett contacted Joy. The ground-breaking date's been set."

I nearly choked. "That's fantastic." Richard Arnett was our attorney. He'd worked so hard with my sisters and me to get construction of a new hospital wing

3

underway. A pediatric center. After my baby brother Nicky died, my parents created the Frost Foundation. My paternal grandpa—a successful land developer—was insanely wealthy. When he passed on, the inheritance was split between my uncle Simon and my father. Mom and Dad promptly earmarked their portion for the center. Now my parents' dreams were going to be realized. I tingled all over. "Did we get the date we'd hoped for—November thirtieth?"

"Yup, Nicky's birthday." Her voice cracked, and I knew her emotions were getting the best of her. "We'll talk more Friday night at dinner. Love ya, Chrissy."

"Love you more." I ended the call and smiled. Grateful tears splashed down my cheeks. Maybe this holiday season wouldn't be so bad after all.

****

"Mr. Hobbs." I fidgeted. My counseling appointments had always been on Tuesdays at noon. I'd sacrificed lunch on those days to allow a gray-haired man with yellow teeth into my head. Ugh! I hated being probed. And I was pretty sure I didn't need it anymore. I'll admit, it helped me in the beginning, but it seemed like a waste of time at this point. Dr. Peterson did not concur with my conclusion.

"What is it, Chrissy?

"Uh, I have an appointment that is usually on Tuesdays at noon, but it's been moved to today at eleven." I didn't want to spill that my appointment—at a clinic nestled in the Colorado hills—was with a head doctor. He might rethink my competence. "May I take my lunch early? If not, I'll cancel—no problem at all." Really, it would be no problem at all.

Mr. Hobbs looked at his appointment book, then

back at me. "That shouldn't be a problem."

"Thank you." I forced a smile.

Eleven o'clock came so much sooner than noon ever did. I stood at the desk in the waiting room behind a rail-thin girl. Anorexia? I always found it fun to play "what's your ailment?" in my head at these appointments. I'd never, until now, realized that the other patients were probably doing the same thing. *Hmm, I wonder what they've come up with for me.*

Finally, the shadow of a girl slipped away, and I approached Linda, the receptionist. I looked at her long, painted fingernails as she punched a few keys on the computer keyboard. I didn't know what she entered. I hadn't given her any new information. It seemed she always had to be typing something. She click, click, clicked as my anxiety rose. I didn't know what it was about being in a shrink's office that put me on edge, but the minute I walked in the door and the smell hit me, I got anxious. It wasn't an unpleasant odor, just something that reminded me of the reason I was here. The sense of smell was powerful that way.

"Hi, Chrissy. You'll be seeing Dr. Brandt today."

I shook my head. "Uh-uh." I shifted my weight toward the door, ready to spring out of there. "I mean, where's Dr. Peterson?" No way did I want to allow another person into my head—especially Dr. Brandt. I was certain the disappointment showed on my face. I'd met Dr. Brandt—bumped into her outside the ladies' room, and she scared me to death. Cold, gray eyes and not a hair out of place—classic scary head shrink.

"Dr. Peterson had to leave town for a family emergency. Turns out, he'll be gone for the rest of the month—or even longer. Sounds pretty bad." She handed me the sign-in clipboard.

"Fine," I mumbled as my shoulders slumped a little. I wrote my name on the line and took a seat in the waiting area.

Pulling out my phone, I used my time wisely by playing a mindless game. Anything to pass the interminably long period it seemed to take to locate a doctor and tell them their patient awaited.

The glass door to the office opened and something changed. Instead of stale memories, the room smelled fresh and clean—like my favorite aftershave. I loved the smell of aftershave. Who smelled so fresh and spicy? I took a deep breath and smiled. I couldn't keep my eyes on the phone. They insisted on following the aroma.

The nice-smelling man spoke to Linda in a caramel smooth voice, and they both laughed. She handed him some papers, and then he took the seat next to mine.

Smooth-voiced-aftershave-wearing man glanced my way.

I sucked in a breath. Something in his chocolate-brown eyes made me want to stare. Who was this guy and why was he seeing a psychiatrist?

I guess I stared long enough he felt the need to speak to me. That, or he was just friendly.

"Hi, I'm Decker."

Yup, caramel smooth. Not that I cared—with my mountain of trust issues. But that didn't mean I wanted to look away.

"Chrissy." I held out a hand for him to shake.

His warm grip sent shivers down my spine.

I pulled my hand away. What had gotten into me? Next thing I knew, I was glancing at the glass on some framed art that decorated the wall behind him, desperate to check my reflection. My long, brunette hair hung in a loose braid over my shoulder, and my hazel eyes shone green. They did that when I wore my favorite jade sweater.

But I didn't know why I cared.

"Are you okay?" He squinted his rich brown eyes at me. Those long, black lashes were such a contrast to his dark blond hair.

I bit down on my lip.

Oh, dear. He smiled, and I realized I'd been in another world.

I gave myself a mental shake. "Yes. I'm fine. Sorry." I wanted to ask him what he was in for, but I knew that would be inappropriate.

"Are you from around here?" His voice vibrated down to my toes.

"Yes. I've lived in Colorado Springs all of my life. I love it here—you know the mountains, the trees…" I was babbling like the brooks I was about to describe so I clamped my mouth shut and again wondered what had gotten into me. Me—the girl who hadn't seriously looked at a man in years. "Uh, what about you, where are you from?"

"I'm from Chicago—you know wind, the weather"—he shivered—"and don't forget the politicians." His lips pulled up into a half smile.

I half melted. I thought I'd built a solid wall around my heart—especially where men were concerned. My sisters' sad track records were enough to keep me single for a lifetime. I didn't know what made this guy different.

"Chrissy, Dr. Brandt is ready to see you," Linda

said in an authoritative voice.

Saved by the receptionist. As gorgeous as he was and as good as he smelled, I didn't trust Decker. I didn't trust any man. Best not let my heart think otherwise.

"Nice to meet you," I mumbled as I stood to follow Linda.

I rounded the corner, leaving the waiting area and that wonderful smell, deep brown eyes, and velvety-smooth voice.

Dr. Brandt motioned for me to follow her into her office.

Like a robot, I did. What else could I do? She was bound to scorch me with her powers of intimidation if I didn't.

"How are you today, Ms. Frost?" She took a seat behind her desk and slid on her reading glasses to look over my file.

I couldn't help but notice the plethora of framed accomplishments and degrees hanging on the wall behind her. Very intimidating. Sometimes I just wanted a friend who'd been through something similar to tell my problems to, not a doctor…especially this doctor.

"Ms. Frost?" She snapped me from my thoughts.

"Oh…I'm…actually…" I ducked my head and rubbed my temples. "I'm sorry, Doctor Brandt." I continued to massage my head. "I feel a migraine coming on. I don't think this is going to work out for me today."

I heard her chuckle. I didn't think Dr. Brandt ever laughed. Wait…*why is she laughing? I'm clearly in pain.*

She pointed to a sticky note attached to my file.

"Dr. Peterson mentioned that you might be resistant to a new caregiver…and were prone to sudden migraines."

How dare he. I felt my whole body blush.

"Your head?" She smiled again and ran a hand through her dark, short-cropped hair.

"Worth a try."

She laughed again.

I realized Dr. Brandt wasn't as bad as I'd imagined. Her eyes twinkled when she smiled, and I even spotted a dimple in her cheek. I never would've guessed.

"Dr. Peterson noted for me to pay special attention to the calendar. It seems ever since your parents' deaths nearly four years ago, winter, particularly the Christmas season, is difficult for you." Her voice was soft and concerned. "That's right around the corner."

I had to look away from those eyes that threatened to peer into my soul. I just couldn't make myself go there with someone new. Not yet.

"I'm sorry, Chrissy. This must be so hard for you. I wish Dr. Peterson were able to be here." She glanced at the calendar. "Especially through the next couple of months. We can talk as much or as little as you want."

Surprisingly, that helped me relax.

We talked about my sisters, baby Nicky, friends, and work. All safe subjects. By the end of the hour, I decided I could get used to this temporary new therapist.

My bladder had threatened to burst during my therapy session, so I paid a visit to the restroom.

When I finished, I stepped out and nearly ran into Linda. "Sorry." I hopped out of the way.

She smiled but continued a conversation she'd obviously started with the other receptionist.

"He's out with Breanna." Linda planted her generous bottom into the ergonomically correct chair and slid up to her computer. After a moment, I was rewarded with the sound of that click, click, click once again.

"Decker's such a nice guy," Kiera, the other receptionist, added.

Wait—they were talking about Decker. I wondered who Breanna was.

"See you next week, Chrissy." Linda waved, pulling me out of my musings.

I smiled and returned her wave.

Well, Decker is obviously taken. Lucky girl. I already disliked this Breanna. She was probably super nice, super skinny, super friendly, super…well, everything good. Like him. And I was broken. After all, I was the reason my parents were dead.

Chapter Two

Back at work, I had plenty to do to keep my mind occupied and off the gorgeous man I'd just met. I hadn't seen a ring on his finger, but it sounded like he at least had a girlfriend. My company had landed an account with Doggone It, a pet boarding and grooming facility.

Mr. Hobbs handed me a thin folder. "You're taking the lead on this one—working with Ashlyn and Cole on advertising."

"Is this the whole file? I mean, it's pretty small." I opened the folder to peruse the material inside.

"The owners didn't give us much in the way of direction. You'll get to use your imagination on this one." He stepped into his office and closed the door.

"It's been nice chatting with you, Mr. Hobbs," I mumbled under my breath. I respected the guy, but occasionally he didn't seem human. He often handed me assignments with little explanation. Sometimes I daydreamed of how his dinner conversations went at home.

Wife: "How was your day?"

Mr. Hobbs: "My day was fine. Pass the potatoes."

Wife: "What did you do today? Anything new?"

Mr. Hobbs: "Use your imagination. Pass the chicken."

Wife: "Well, my day was fantastic. I met an Italian

weightlifter at the gym, and we spent the day fulfilling my every fantasy. Isn't that nice, dear?"

Mr. Hobbs: "Glad you had a good time. Pass the peas."

I giggled. Sometimes I thought I was so funny. I probably wasn't. But at least I kept myself entertained.

The floor I worked on at Hobbs and Bevins Marketing Firm was a maze of desks partitioned off to create separate cubicles. A bank of private offices lined the east wall, and if you walked down the hall from there, you'd dead-end into a conference room.

I scooted through the desks until I found my own and spread the paperwork out in front of me. An assignment like this one for the pet facility would be tricky. These types of clients wanted us to read their minds. They claimed we had free rein to do whatever we thought was best, until we went ahead—and they hated it. I'd learned to start by dipping my toe in the water. Instead of spending monumental amounts of time on one fantastic idea that may or may not be what the client wanted, I pulled a few thoughts together and waited for their reaction. I was a bit compulsive, so when I got the idea I knew would knock their socks off, I wanted to dive in head first. This job had taught me to slow down. It also taught me that not everyone had superior taste like I did, and that was just something I'd have to live with.

After looking over the file details—budget, deadlines, etc.—I found Ashlyn and Cole to set up a meeting. We needed to break things down and divvy up the assignments. Ashlyn had always been great to work with—dependable and creative—but Cole...let's just say Cole was sort of an Adonis type. He was drop-dead gorgeous—and he knew it. He skated by on his good looks and charm. I didn't know how his parents knew to name him Cole, but somehow they did. It totally suited him. He had coal black hair and cobalt blue eyes. When he smiled, his delicious dimples made you want to kiss him.

I had kissed him—more than once. He was a decent kisser, but it hadn't been everything I'd hoped for. Maybe it hadn't been the kiss, but the kisser I'd not cared for. We'd dated for a while when we first met. Yes, I fell for his good looks and charm, like every other girl. But it hadn't taken long for me to realize that, while Cole was a nice guy, I wanted a man with more substance. Perhaps if I'd met him before my parents died, it may have ended differently—or not at all—but I'd like to think I've grown up a bit since then. My values had definitely matured. Tragedy forced you to grow up, whether you wanted to or not.

At any rate, Cole and I still got along fine. He'd flirt with me every once in a while, but he was never offended when I ignored him.

I wondered what kind of kisser Decker was. His gorgeous face, spicy smell, and smooth voice floated through my mind and paused there just long enough to distract me.

"Ahem." Cole nudged my arm.

"Oh, right. Sorry." I gave myself a mental shake. It wasn't like me to daydream—especially about a man I just met—and was possibly taken.

The three of us huddled together. Ashlyn, with her swollen belly, scooted as close to the conference table as she could get.

"Looking round and cute there," I said. "Feeling

okay?"

"Fat and sassy." She patted her tummy.

A silent moment passed as we all perused the papers in front of us.

Ashlyn's mouth turned downward into a frown and a wrinkle creased her brow.

I knew what she was thinking. "You're due at the same time as our deadline, huh?" This wasn't good news.

"Yeah. It looks that way. Maybe I can get my part done early. Of course, with Thanksgiving and Christmas…" Her voice trailed off.

We both looked at Cole. He shrugged. "We can handle it, Chrissy." He punched my arm. "You do your best work under pressure." He winked.

Yes, but you don't. I wanted to scream back. "Sure, we'll be fine. Don't worry." We had no choice. Everyone else at the firm had other assignments.

The thought of all the extra work I potentially had in my future should have made me anxious, but during the fall and upcoming holiday season, I welcomed diversions from life. Keeping busy took my mind off the reason I still visited with Dr. Peterson, or now Dr. Brandt, every week. Yes, I could bury myself in my work as well as anyone. And for this assignment, I would have to.

By Friday night, I was ready for the weekend. My sisters and I had plans to meet at The Mason Jar, our favorite restaurant. We'd been doing this for years. Not every Friday, but whenever we could all coordinate our schedules.

"Holly," I called out. She sat on a wooden bench nestled next to a black and red checkerboard wall in the waiting area. Country music played in the background.

She jumped out of her seat and pulled me in for a hug. "Anyone else here yet?" I asked.

"Nope, just me."

Holly was almost always the first to arrive. She didn't have any children to leave with a sitter like Joy and Elle, and she lived pretty close to the restaurant. Sometimes I wished my niece and nephews would tag along with their moms. I absolutely adored them, but we sisters needed our girl time.

We made small talk as we waited for the others. I loved chatting with Holly one-on-one. When we were all together, she tended to quietly listen and let the rest of us do the talking. She had always been the patient one in the family. And the peacemaker—never wanting to make waves. I'd say she was almost too patient. Only because she was twenty-eight and still single. There was nothing wrong with that, but Holly was gorgeous, and there were many men who'd love to change her relationship status to "taken," but she only had eyes for one guy—Elam. They broke it off a while back, but I didn't think she'd ever recovered. She worked as a nurse, like my mom did. I hoped a nice doctor stole her heart someday.

Elle came next, and the hostess seated us at a booth near the front, so we'd be able to flag Joy down when she arrived.

Finally, the door of The Mason Jar flew open and in blew Joy…and…who in the world—

I sucked in a breath. Could it be…Uncle Simon? I hadn't seen him since I was a young teenager.

Elle, Holly, and I wore the same confused expressions.

Joy finally realized he'd entered behind her and spoke up. "Look who showed up at my house." She tugged on his arm. Her smile radiant.

He nodded as if waiting for our approval.

"Oh, you look just like Dad," I blurted out.

Noelle and Holly held back, but I wrapped my arms around him, relishing his warmth and thoughts of my father.

He smiled at me, his tense-looking posture relaxed, and he hugged the others. "You are all so lovely."

What a classy man.

I slid back onto my seat. "It's so good to see you, Uncle Simon." My spirit soared.

He chuckled and I nearly wept. His voice, his blue eyes, and that smile all belonged to my dad. He mentioned he'd bought a condo and would be moving back to the Springs.

I clapped my hands together. "That's wonderful. We hope to see a lot of you, don't we?" I glanced around at my sisters.

I was disappointed when Uncle Simon declined dinner, saying he had a meeting to get to. Before leaving, he told me how much I resembled my mom, which meant the world to me.

I looked forward to learning more about him and where he'd been. I was a kid when I saw him last, and my parents rarely mentioned his name. Strange. He and my dad seemed so much alike.

My sisters all had different opinions about the sudden arrival of Uncle Simon—some happy, some suspicious. I chose to believe he was here because someone upstairs knew I needed my dad back.

****

I climbed out of my car a few minutes before my therapy session was scheduled to begin the next Wednesday. Dr. Brandt's office was in a medical professional complex, and as I began my ascent up the stairs to the office of "brain examination," the door next to the clinic opened and a cute guy came out.

He smiled, but only half his face pulled up.

I suppressed a laugh. Clearly the guy had been to see the dentist and was under the effects of Novocain.

"Hello," he said.

"Hi." I averted my eyes, still trying not to laugh.

He did his best to flirt, but I couldn't get over the paralyzed face. As he attempted to keep the conversation going, I looked for an escape.

"I'm sorry," I said. "I've got an appointment, um, here." With a twinge of embarrassment, I pointed limply at the door to the clinic. The upturned side of his smile fell. I felt bad for brushing him off, but not bad enough to stay and chat. "Have a good day."

He nodded, and we parted ways.

I saw Dr. Brandt standing behind Linda, holding some papers. When I walked in, they greeted me in unison. I would be so happy when I could enter a doctor's office and feel like a stranger again. Soon, it would be soon.

I took my usual seat across from the doctor.

"Does that happen often?"

"What?" I tilted my head. "Does what happen often?"

"When you arrived today, you were stopped by a man who clearly had an interest in you."

"You saw that?"

"The front door is glass. Not difficult to see. It also

didn't escape my notice that you didn't return his interest. I wondered if that happens often."

I narrowed my eyes. "Is this a trick question?"

She chuckled. "No, it's not. I've just been reading your relationship history and see that you don't—"

"Have one." I cut her off, embarrassed to admit that I didn't have anyone in my life to run off to lunch dates with or come home to at night. It wasn't that I didn't want one—I did. I'd longed for the right guy to come into my life, but somehow there had always been a bump in the road where men were concerned.

"I wasn't going to say that. You're still young and don't need to feel pressured. However, Dr. Peterson noted that you have a distinct pattern where relationships are concerned. Having a man in your life isn't going to fix you, Chrissy, but I wonder if perhaps dissecting your relationship problems will help with some of your coping skills."

I lifted my shoulders in a non-committal maybe.

"You are an attractive, vibrant young lady, and according to this, you haven't had any real relationships since—"

"My freshman year in college." Wow. I couldn't believe it'd been nearly six years ago. I suddenly felt lonely.

"Chrissy, what are you afraid of?"

"Well, my parents loved each other and had a wonderful marriage—until they were killed in a car accident. My oldest sister loved her husband and was fulfilled and happy—until he died serving our country. Another of my sisters married the man she thought would give her the moon—but instead he gave her a lot of deep emotional scars, then a divorce after she caught him cheating. And finally, I have a sister who is in love with a man who doesn't give her the time of day. Wouldn't you think twice before diving into a serious relationship if you were me?"

She laid the folder down and looked at me for what seemed like a full minute before she finally spoke. "Chrissy," she said, "all of those facts are here in your paperwork—almost word for word. Dig deeper. What are you really afraid of?"

I thought those were pretty good reasons to avoid relationships—that is, if she was even right about me. I'd mentally listed those things so many times in my head that I believed they were true. No wonder I hadn't sounded sincere or convincing. But surely she was wrong. After all, I'd been attracted to that cute guy, Decker, in the waiting room. Well, one short encounter didn't count. Maybe…could there be more to my emotional detachment from relationships than I even realized? I studied my fingernails while I pondered.

She sat patiently waiting. "Think back to the last time you began to feel something for someone. What triggered you to back off?"

I closed my eyes and did what she asked. Yes. I could see a pattern in my relationships, and it had always been me who ended them. The last one had been a year ago. Things had gone so well with Dustin Jones until…until…

It hit me—I had refused to admit the truth all this time. A lump grew in my throat.

"I think…" My voice sounded feeble, even to me. I cleared my throat. Tears stung my eyes as the truth came into vision. "I think I sabotage my relationships when they get too serious because of that." I motioned to my file.

"Because you've been coming here for help? That shows strength, not weakness. It means you see a problem and are willing to fix it."

"No, not because I come here. Because of the *reason* I come here. Nobody wants to be involved with someone who tried to commit suicide." I felt a burden lift from actually saying the words.

Dr. Brandt shifted in her chair. "Chrissy, look at me."

I raised my eyes. Her face looked blurry through my tears. When she handed me a tissue, I wanted to grab her hand—something to hold onto; someone to hold onto.

"What you went through was extremely traumatic. Taking pills to find an escape from the pain doesn't make you unlovable. If anything, it speaks to how much you loved your parents, and how much you need love."

Wow. Right to the bottom of my dark time to my deepest regret.

Dr. Peterson had probably tried, but never succeeded in convincing me I'd shown some sort of need for taking those pills. No, I'd always felt inferior, weak. So much so that I'd punished myself ever since by pushing away good men because I didn't deserve them.

"I only did it once. I knew there were better ways to deal with their deaths—but I needed...I...needed to disappear." I dabbed at my tears. "I really am so much stronger now."

"Strong enough to enter a relationship?" She smiled and raised her eyebrows.

I shrugged. "I guess I won't know until Mister

Right comes along. And that guy outside, he was not Mister Right."

We both laughed.

"Chrissy, you don't have to wait around for the perfect man to ask you out. There are no perfect men. No perfect women, either. But there's nothing wrong with asking someone out, if you're interested in him."

Hmm. I'd always let the men do the asking.

After a few more loaded questions and even heavier answers, my counseling session was over.

"Thank you."

"For?" She scooped up the papers and put them neatly back into my folder.

"For making me dig deeper."

I thought she'd say something cliché, like "just doing my job." But instead she smiled and said, "There are probably a dozen guys out there in need of therapy because you dumped them."

I laughed out loud. Her words caught me totally off guard.

She chuckled, too, but then became serious. "Really, Chrissy, don't sell yourself short. You're so much more than a file of past sorrows and mistakes." She nodded to my folder, then nodded to me. "See you next week."

I left Dr. Brandt's office feeling lighter than I had in years. That was when it hit me—the sound of caramel deliciousness. I stopped in my tracks and sniffed. Yup, no mistaking; spicy freshness filled the air.

"Chrissy?"

Chapter Three

I erased the dream-like expression I was sure I was wearing and tried to look surprised.

"Oh, hi. Decker, is it?" I acted nonchalant but couldn't help but wonder why he was back here where the doctors hung out. I thought he was a patient, like me. Maybe he'd just finished his appointment.

His warm eyes twinkled.

I opened my mouth to say something clever. "Uh…do you want to go out to dinner sometime?" The words tumbled out before I realized what I'd done. I fidgeted while all logic became scrambled in my brain. "Like, eat something…stuff…food?" *Ack. Stop, Chrissy.* Dr. Brandt must have cast some kind of spell on me. I was never so forward. Heat rose to my face. I thought I might pass out.

Silence.

Oh, jellybeans. He's probably a doctor and I put him in an awkward position. "Um—" I started to shake my head.

He looked around, then motioned me to follow him to an open room.

For a long moment I stood rooted in place, wondering if I could dash out the front door, but his reassuring smile urged me to join him.

He stood so close to me; I could hardly think straight. Sure, he smelled wonderful and his voice flowed like smooth caramel, but those eyes—those intense brown eyes—they nearly undid me.

I gave him a confused look.

He chuckled. "Sorry, I didn't want the whole staff to hear our conversation."

"Wait, do you work here?"

His smile faltered; then a look of understanding seemed to creep into his expression. "No. I don't work here. However, I do research for my thesis on Mondays, Wednesdays, and Fridays here. Is that a problem?"

Hmm, I didn't know if that was a problem. Such a scenario I hadn't considered. I'd been ready to rescind my offer—beautiful eyes and all—if he were a doctor. I didn't need someone else in my head. However, Dr. Brandt's challenge to enter a new relationship armed with fresh resolve echoed in my mind.

I twisted my fingers together.

"So, dinner?" he said.

I snapped out of my internal debate. "Yeah. You know, if you want to." My heart thudded, and I became more and more unsure of myself by the second. "I just thought…" What? What had I thought? That I could go up to a nearly perfect stranger and he'd fall all over himself to go out with me?

"Sure, I'd love to."

I shrugged. "That's okay. I'll see you late—" Before I completely backed out the of the room and out of my request for a date, I realized what he'd said.

His eyes sparkled with amusement.

My face burned. *He must think I'm an idiot.*

Unsure of my next move as the date initiator, I turned my phone over and over in my hands. "Great. So—"

He chuckled. "How about Friday night?"

I let out a breath. "Sounds good. Thanks."

We exchanged numbers.

He flashed a heart-melting smile, then left.

I looked at my feet. Heart-melting smile? *Chrissy, get ahold of yourself. Dr. Brandt said to enter a relationship, not turn to mush in front of the first man I meet.*

I ambled over to the front desk, giving Decker plenty of time to be on his way. Then I waited for Linda to finish typing more info, from who-knows-where, into her computer. "So, Linda, what's the story with Decker? Why is he here all the time?" I knew she had to keep quiet about other patients, but not researchers.

Linda looked at the ceiling as if the answers were written there, then back down at me. "He comes here to do research. I think he's gone to medical school and has everything completed except for his residency." She stopped.

I wondered why she stopped. And I wondered why he stopped. "And? Why didn't he do his residency?"

"Oh, that's where I'm not real clear. Something happened, and he had to take a break."

Duh. Come on—think, Linda. I wanted to give her a good shake. Did I have a chance with him or not?

"I can't remember the details, but I think he still plans on finishing. I'll have to ask Kiera. She made him tell her the whole story when he started coming here."

Grr. I'll have to buddy up with Kiera, I guess.

"Oh, it's too bad he had to quit." I turned toward the door, disappointed in her lack of Decker details. "Well, thanks for the info. I've got to run."

The car ride back to the office was a noisy one—in

my head, at least. My brain argued that just because Decker didn't have the title yet, he was still off limits—too close to being a therapist. My heart countered with the sincerity I'd seen in his eyes, the way I'd tingled all over when he was near, and of course Dr. Brandt's challenge.

Both heart and head were being quite stubborn. Then my stomach growled, trumping all. I pulled into a Taco Bell drive-through to satisfy at least one of the voices.

When I returned to work, Cole and Ashlyn were singing a jingle they'd been working on for Doggone It. It involved fake dogs and cats making indistinguishable noises that made me want to turn tail and leave. Rush back to Decker—but Decker wouldn't be there.

"Chrissy, listen to our jingle," Cole said when he caught sight of me.

"Oh, I have been. I think half the city could hear those howling noises."

Cole chuckled. His dimples puckered, and his eyes sparkled. "Come on, Ashlyn, let's sing it for her."

They proceeded to serenade me with more of those awful noises.

"Stop. I can't take it."

"Those will be real cats and dogs, Chrissy. We're messing around right now."

I blew out a breath, relieved my coworkers hadn't completely lost all their jellybeans—something my dad used to say. "So where are we on the media advertisements?"

Ashlyn brought me up to speed, and we all got back to work.

Mr. Hobbs stalked out of his office. He turned his

head this way and that, then stopped when he spotted me.

A scowl marred his features. Evidently, he and Mr. Bevins had been in an intense meeting. The look on his face didn't bode well for what I feared was coming next.

"Chrissy, the deadline for Doggone It moved up. They want it finished before Christmas, so everyone can take a break over the holiday."

"That's three weeks earlier than the original date." My voice rose. "We can't pull a full marketing strategy together that fast."

"You'll have to. We lost the Tammy's Tacos account and we can't afford to lose another one."

I would have asked him how we were supposed to accomplish such a big assignment in such a short time, but I knew what he'd say, "Use your imagination."

I turned to Ashlyn and Cole, who both stood there with gaping mouths.

"Well, you heard the man. We'd better get going. I'll work on graphics. Ashlyn, you keep revising the media spots, and, Cole, fix that jingle for the television ads. It's way too cheesy—even with real animals."

Cole looked genuinely hurt, but I didn't have time to soothe egos. We had less than two months to complete four months of work.

"And tomorrow we're taking a tour of their facility. It's so much easier to sell something you can stand behind." I crossed my fingers that we could stand behind it.

****

The next morning, bright and early, we entered the Doggone It Boarding and Grooming facility. The smell was a pungent mix of animal feces and wet dog. I had to cover my nose. My heart sank. We couldn't promote a business that fell short of their claim to care for their clients' animals. No one in their right mind would board their pets here now. I wondered why any were here at all.

The owner, Mrs. Teague, had to be pushing ninety. Okay, that was an exaggeration; she was probably more like seventy. I found it hard to tell with the huge amount of lipstick and blush she wore. Regardless of her appearance, she did look too old to be running an establishment like this. She wore enormous hearing aids, and her glasses swung from a chain around her neck. The fine little wisp of bleached blonde hair that clung for dear life atop her angular head stuck straight up.

"Mrs. Teague, I'm Christina Frost. We're here from Hobbs and Bevins Marketing Firm."

"What's that?" Her cigarette bobbed up and down, stuck to her lips as she spoke.

I introduced myself again. Louder this time.

Some of the dogs began to howl.

She fiddled with her hearing aid. "Oh...oh, yes. You're the ones we hired to do some marketin' for us."

I looked around to see who "us" would include.

"Yes, ma'am. Can I ask why you moved the deadline up? It's going to be difficult to get a decent campaign together in such a short time."

Her eyes flashed, and I could tell that, just that fast, she'd become defensive. "I d'know why it should be s'hard to figure somethin' out. Yer perfessionals, aren't ya?"

"Yes, ma'am." *I guess that question will go*

unanswered.

"Show everyone how we love animals. Everybody looooves animals." She arched her eyebrows as she drew out the word "loves."

Everyone but you, evidently. I looked around, desperate to find some redeeming quality at Doggone It. Something to run with.

Mrs. Teague waved her speckled hand toward the cages. "Them animals are long-termers. That's what we call 'em. When their owners come t'claim 'em, I won't have no more ta take care of. I need more business. No one's been bringin' their pets here lately."

I couldn't imagine why. I glanced at Cole and Ashlyn. They both studied their feet.

Thanks, guys.

"Okay, Mrs. Teague. We need to look around and then we'll be out of your hair." Probably a bad choice of words, since she hardly had any.

I snapped some pictures of the dirty kennels and some of the unhappy dogs and cats, which didn't add up to very many pets, then whispered to Cole, "Let's get out of here before we catch something."

He nodded, and we left.

The drive back to the office was silent. None of us knew how we could represent this company. Yet neither did we know how to break the news to Mr. Hobbs. The firm needed the business.

I loved dogs. Our dog, Lucky, had grown up with me, and when he died, I mourned for months. I'd have a dog now, but pets weren't allowed in my apartment. Even if they were, Kassandra, my roommate, was allergic. I'd hated seeing those poor neglected animals at Doggone It. They deserved to be cared for—cleaned, exercised. They looked fed, but unhappy.

****

—We still on for dinner Friday night?— My finger shook as I pressed the send text button. My pulse raced at the thought of a date with Decker, but it had been no easy task working up the nerve to ask. Guilt pinched at my conscience for all the dates I'd turned down in the past. I never imagined how difficult it was to be the initiator.

My phone chirped almost immediately.—*Chrissy, want to go shopping before dinner Friday night? I need new clothes. I wonder if Uncle Simon will be crashing the party again.*—

I stared at my phone before the realization hit that I was reading a text from my sister, Holly. I laughed until I put two and two together. Yikes. I forgot. Friday night I had a girls' night with my sisters planned. Frost sisters' girls' nights were sacred—once they were on the calendar, no one messed with them. Plus, we needed to tie up any loose ends for the hospital wing groundbreaking.

I hurried to text Decker.—*Oops, slipped my mind. I have something Friday night, but I'm free for lunch almost any day.*— I'm such an airhead. I paced my bedroom waiting for a reply…from Decker, not Holly.

—*I'm sorry, lunch doesn't work for me.*—He finally wrote back.

Ever? Lunch wouldn't work for him ever? No explanation; that was all he wrote. I wasn't usually the jealous type, but sudden feelings of envy and suspicion crept into my heart. I bet he'd read my file and regretted ever agreeing to a date in the first place. Why did I even ask him?

Chapter Four

For the rest of the week I spent every waking moment working on something for the Doggone It campaign, which was good—it kept my mind off Decker. I would come up with an idea, then scrap it and start over again. Besides not being able to find the right fit for the terrible place, something bothered me about the owner. I couldn't imagine why someone who obviously didn't like animals owned a pet facility. Things didn't add up. I shook my head for the hundredth time.

I posed my concerns to my roommate Kassie. Most people who knew us both called her Kassandra. I guessed Chrissy and Kassie were too similar. Sounded like twins. We'd been friends since college and had a lot in common, but there were differences, too. For instance, I was tidy—or at least I thought I was—but she was a neat-freak. She didn't seem to mind when I left a dish in the sink now and then, and I didn't complain too much when she incessantly cleaned— sometimes taking the dish I was still using right out from under my fork and sticking it in the dishwasher. I thought it was second nature to her—it drove her crazy to see anything out of place. She was a good listener, and I'd bent her ear a lot this week. I was feeling desperate about the Doggone It campaign.

"Why don't you just refuse to do it, Chrissy?" She

pulled a tray of nachos out of the microwave for a late-night snack.

The smell of warm, melted cheese wafted through the air, making my mouth water. "I can't. Our firm needs the business. We've lost a couple of big clients lately." I reached for a chip and popped it in my mouth. "Ouch. Watch out—they're sizzling hot."

Kassie tucked a piece of light brown hair behind her ear and narrowed her blue eyes. "But if you can't represent the company honestly, how can you build a campaign?" She was smart and blew puffs of air on her chip before eating it. In fact, Kassie was definitely the logical type. Everything was black and white to her. Unfortunately, in the marketing industry we had to blur the lines sometimes to make things work.

Something she'd said stuck with me for the next few days, though. I agreed with her about making our campaign honest. I just didn't know how to do it. And what about that horrid woman, Mrs. Teague? She screamed, "Fake! Fake! Fake!" to me. I didn't know how to make something honest that wasn't. I blew out a frustrated breath.

Someone else spoke to me, too—a kind, gentle voice. "Never judge a book by its cover." Yup, my mom. Gone nearly four years, but still whispering words of wisdom to me. Her soft voice rang the loudest in my ears.

On an impulse, I dialed Mrs. Teague's number the next morning.

"Hello?" Her raspy voice made it clear I woke her up.

Now what? Maybe I should hang up and let her get some more beauty rest. No, those animals needed to be fed. "Hi, Mrs. Teague. This is Christina Frost from Hobbs and Bevins. I thought it might be nice to chat about some marketing ideas over lunch this week. Do you have time? My treat, of course," I was quick to add.

She cleared her throat. "Well…uh…let me check my calendar."

I imagined her staring at the ceiling and counting to ten.

"It looks like I can squeeze you in…uh, tomorrow?"

I let out a breath of relief. "Yes, that's great. I'll pick you up at noon." We ended the call. I bit my bottom lip. Now I worried about what I'd find to discuss with her. Sometimes my impulsiveness got the better of me. But I needed to know what made this client tick.

Lunchtime on Tuesday came quickly. I picked Mrs. Teague up and we drove to The Mason Jar—the one place I knew the wait staff, should things go south, and I needed some kind of emotional support—like a phone call that would rush me back to the office. I could count on them.

Mrs. Teague had fashioned her thin hair into tight curls. They almost covered the bald spots. Her makeup was still gaudy, but the cigarette was gone—thank goodness. I was rather shocked to see she wore clothing better suited for a twenty-year-old—tight and revealing. A hot pink, scoop-necked t-shirt exposed her wrinkled cleavage, while a short denim skirt barely covered her legs. I couldn't figure her out, but I was determined to try.

Along with the hairdo, makeup, and tight clothes, she also wore that familiar façade—the I'm-superior-smarter-can-handle-anything-don't-cross-me face she'd worn at her pet facility.

Hmm, I've got to work out how to get past that, I thought as I sat down across from her.

****

"It was the strangest thing. This woman, who looks like a seventy-year-old hooker, is the most unique person." I didn't know why, but I could hardly contain my excitement when I talked to Dr. Brandt about my lunch with Mrs. Teague.

She was kind enough to act interested. "How so?"

"Well, she was so prickly when I picked her up, but the minute I treated her like a friend instead of a client, that icy exterior began to melt. She didn't completely thaw and warm to me, but I made real progress." Any progress was a victory to me.

Dr. Brandt didn't say anything, so I went on. "I guess it's important for me to figure her out, so I can discover why she owns a pet facility when she clearly doesn't care a jellybean about animals." Another of my dad's lines. He used jellybeans to express several emotions. I smiled as I pictured him saying it.

Dr. Brandt chuckled. "I think maybe you should be the one wearing this." She motioned to her white lab coat.

I turned my smile to her. "I think maybe she's lonely. And I know she needs help out there. I'm going to see if my team is willing to spend a few hours Saturday cleaning up the place."

Her eyebrows shot skyward. "You're going to fix up the pet facility?"

"Are you doing that parroting thing again?"

She smirked. "No. I just think it's kind of

remarkable that you're willing to help her out like that."

"Someone's got to take care of those animals—not to mention, my job could be on the line if I don't figure out an advertising campaign." I tucked some hair behind my ear. "Okay, Doctor, I've gone on long enough. It's your turn. I'm ready to be shrunk." I closed my eyes and allowed her to enter my brain.

When she didn't say anything, I looked up. She was reading something in my file. "Oh no. What have you found now?"

"You went through college on a full-ride scholarship?"

I blanched—not what I had expected to hear. "Why, do only stupid people attempt suicide?" I felt a wall erecting.

"No, no. Actually, it's quite the opposite. But that's not what surprised me. I apologize if it came across that way. What I mean is, how did you get through school, maintaining grades required to keep a full-ride scholarship, after what happened to your parents?"

"Oh." I let myself relax and step back off the soapbox I'd found myself mounting. "That would be Joy, Noelle, and Holly."

She laughed. "Sounds like a Christmas carol."

"Close. They're my sisters. They refused to let me quit school and they've been quite vigilant about never letting me skip therapy sessions. They can be pushy when it comes to me. As the youngest of the family, I am both pampered and bossed."

"Sounds like some pretty great sisters. Why the Christmas names?"

"My parents were funny that way. They were married in March around thirty-five years ago, and all of us girls have December birthdays. We all came to the conclusion—March had been a very cozy anniversary month for them. Then, to emphasize the fact that we all had December birthdays, lest anyone forget, they gave us holiday names: Joy, Noelle, Holly, and me, Chrissy. My baby brother Nick came a bit early, but Mom didn't want him to be left out."

I couldn't keep the smile from my face as memories of my somewhat cheesy parents emerged.

Mom had been my best friend. She'd worked as a nurse. Not one of those stodgy nurses who looked down her nose at you through round-framed spectacles. No, my mom had been a "hip" nurse—if there were such a thing. And she always made time for her baby girl—me. When I'd gone off to college at the University of Colorado in Boulder, I was pretty sure I stretched the umbilical cord the entire distance. We used to talk on the phone daily. Until we didn't.

My memories took a sour turn. I realized I was frowning when Dr. Brandt's voice shook me from my trance. "Your parents sound delightful." Her eyes twinkled, and I forced a smile.

"They were." Too bad they died as a direct result of my actions. My eyes burned. I squeezed them closed to push out the memory. No one, not even my sisters, knew what had really happened that day.

Conversation moved to my job. Nothing sad about that. In fact, talking about it sparked my enthusiasm for what I did.

The second my session ended, I was the first one up and sprinting toward the door, excited to get back to work and construct a plan to rehabilitate the Doggone It pet facility. I turned and told her, "Thanks. See ya next week."

I swung the glass door of the medical facility open and got as far as the second step, when a frigid gust of air nearly knocked me off my feet. I clung to the railing and my limbs stiffened. I didn't know how this could happen. Panic clawed at me. When I'd come in for my appointment, the sun was shining. Although the air had been chilly, it had still been autumn an hour before. Now winter had bullied its way in. I couldn't move—paralyzed. A snowflake landed on my nose. I had to disappear. That uncomfortable darkness was moving into my soul.

I heard a voice, but it garbled up in my head. I turned to run back into the building—somewhere safe.

"Chrissy?"

I tried to suck in a breath. I couldn't. And someone was yelling at me.

"Chrissy!"

"It's winter. It's snowing. They're gone. My parents are gone."

I ran smack into the voice that called my name. He wouldn't let me pass.

"Chrissy." Decker's arms closed around me. I couldn't quit shaking. "You're having a panic attack."

Chapter Five

Dizziness overtook me, and I was so thankful he was there to keep me from falling down those cement stairs.

He held me with one arm and wrapped his fur-lined jacket around me with the other. "Looks like you forgot your coat. Winter arrived while we weren't looking."

"Thank you," I managed to squeak out. "You...you've got...lunch, or something." My teeth chattered.

"I'm not going anywhere until I know you're okay." He took out his phone and punched in a text. "There's a coffee shop around the corner. Can I take you there? We could get something warm to drink. Deep breaths." He tightened his grip around me. "I've got you."

I didn't know if I answered him. My head wasn't clear. I only knew that a few minutes later I ended up sitting in a booth across from Decker, sipping a cup of hot cocoa.

He regarded me with those intense brown eyes. I thought he was waiting for me to croak any moment— turn belly-up and die. He wore a button-down plaid shirt and jeans. And he smelled like the spicy freshness I'd come to know as his scent.

"I'm really sorry about that. I don't know what happened. I'm sure I'll be okay, if you want to go...you should go." Still frazzled, all my concentration went into forming coherent sentences.

He shook his head. "No. I don't want to go. Does this happen to you often?"

I said no at the same time I nodded yes.

He chuckled.

"It happened a lot after my parents' accident."

He tilted his head and lowered his brows. "Can I ask what happened to them?"

A whoosh left my body. I didn't know why I assumed he knew about the tragic accident that claimed my parents' lives. I guess I thought everyone associated with Mountainside Medical knew my history and judged me because of my reaction and inability to cope. What a relief.

Decker had seen the worst of me standing paralyzed on the steps of the clinic. Somehow that made it easier to recite the whole tale—leaving out the one thing I'll go to my grave with. No one needed to know my parents died doing something on my behalf. I hoped he was sincere in his desire to hear it, because I spilled, and hardly took a breath.

He never interrupted me, but his eyes spoke volumes. At one point, I swore he even got teary. When I told him about my suicide attempt—yup, I went there—I fully expected to see revulsion in his eyes. Instead, he pulled my hand into his, which sent a mass of tingles to my toes.

"I've since learned to stay in during snowstorms. This one took me by surprise." I looked at my watch. "Oh, no. I've got to get back to work. I've been gone for two hours." I tried to stand, but he pulled me back down.

"You should call your work and tell them you aren't feeling well. I think it's best if you take the rest of the day off—or at least wait out the storm."

As I began to protest, he gently took my chin and turned my face toward the outside window. The snowflakes had tripled in size and now blanketed the street. I felt the blood drain from my face. "But what about you?"

"I have nothing else today. I was just going to catch up on organizing my files. I'm not leaving you alone while you're having this reaction to the snow."

Wow—gorgeous and so nice, too.

"Are we going to stay here until it stops snowing? That could be midnight or next Tuesday." I smiled, but I knew I looked pathetic.

He glanced around, then pointed out the window. "There's a theater across the street. How about we go to a movie? After all, you did promise me a date." He winked.

I didn't have time to react to my erratically beating heart, because he was still talking.

"That way you can forget it's snowing outside, and if it's stormy when we leave, I'll take you home, or to one of your sisters' houses. I don't think you should be alone."

Past experience taught me he was right. Being alone during one of my attacks only intensified my reaction. "You mean you'll take me where I'm not screaming about it being winter on the steps of a medical center?" I smiled again so he'd know I could laugh at myself. This time I hoped I looked normal.

He let out a breath and returned my smile. "So how about it?"

"Okay, but I'm buying the popcorn, since your files are going to be disorganized because of me."

I called work, then used the powder room. The mirror wasn't my friend. I touched up my makeup and ran a brush through my hair. Better.

In order to avoid a holiday show, we ended up going to a romantic comedy I'd never heard of. I didn't care what we saw; I was just glad to be out of the snow. On a weekday and mid-afternoon, the theater was mostly empty. We sat square in the middle. Armed with popcorn and soda, we were ready.

I thought I was doing pretty well. The hot cocoa had helped, but when I reached for some popcorn, my fingers still shook. "Why is it so cold in movie theaters?" I asked, blaming the thermostat instead of my mixed-up head. "You're probably freezing, since I'm still wearing your coat."

He shrugged. "I'm fine."

I tucked my hands under my legs to keep them from shaking.

"But you're clearly not. Give me your hands."

I inclined my head and gave him a questioning look but pulled my rattling fingers out and put them in front of him. He raised the armrest between us and took both of them into his warm, large hands. He gently massaged some circulation back into them. Now I felt warm all over—tingly, too. I knew he was being a gentleman/friend, but I couldn't help but wonder how it would feel if he were my boyfriend. For now, I would enjoy being in a dark theater, sitting close to a good-looking, nice-smelling man.

The show was a silly comedy. We both laughed, despite the inane plot line. I needed to laugh.

By the time the movie ended, the snow had, as well. Darkness had fallen, and the moon lit the clear sky. The roads were a bit slushy. Deliciously perfect Decker drove me to my car, then followed behind me to my apartment to make sure I arrived home safely.

I rolled down my window. "I need to give you your coat."

"Bring it to the clinic. I have another one. Have a good night."

"You, too. And thanks so much."

He waved, then drove away.

As soon as I walked into the apartment, Kassie had all kinds of questions. I didn't want to talk—just remember.

"I'll tell you about it tomorrow, Kass." I yawned. "I'm going to bed now."

"It's not even seven o'clock yet. Have you eaten dinner?"

Come to think of it, the only things I'd eaten since breakfast were cocoa, soda, and popcorn.

"I made some mac and cheese, if you're hungry," she said.

My stomach growled.

"Thanks, Kass. I guess I am hungry. But no questions about the snow, because, well, you know"—and she did—"and I'm not taking off this coat, no matter how warm it is."

Her eyes grew wide, but she didn't say a word—just raised her brows.

We both giggled and filled big bowls of our all-time-favorite comfort food.

"By the way, your uncle…uh, Steven…"

"Simon," I said.

"Yes. Your Uncle Simon stopped by. He said to give you this." She handed me a business card. "He said to call him for a lunch date sometime."

I smiled and pocketed the card. "Thanks, Kass."

My sisters and I hadn't seen much of Uncle Simon since he arrived in Colorado, but I adored him. He was absolutely charming. I didn't know why Dad hadn't talked about him very often. I guess it was because Uncle Simon never lived nearby. It was a shame. They really were alike.

I wandered to my room, in search of my bed.

As much as I didn't want to analyze what had happened earlier that afternoon, I couldn't sleep without doing just that. First, Decker was not a therapist—pro. Second, Decker planned on becoming a therapist—con. Third, I didn't trust men because I was afraid they'd run when they heard about my history of handling traumatic situations—con. Fourth, Decker didn't run—pro. Fifth, I didn't know why he didn't run—perhaps he was just being polite—probably a con. Sixth, he either had a girlfriend or was some kind of player, because when we compared schedules, his lunch hour was always spoken for and he never said why. But I knew, and I thought her name was Breanna—definitely a con.

When the cons began outnumbering the pros, my heart grew heavy and so did my eyelids. Wrapped in the warmth of a spicy-fresh smelling jacket, I finally gave in to the drowsiness.

****

"You want us to go where and do what?" Cole's frown I'd expected, but I thought Ashlyn would be more onboard with my plan.

"Well, how else do you expect us to promote a

42

business that's gone to the dogs?" I couldn't help but laugh at my own corny pun.

The other two didn't even crack a smile.

"Listen, I know cleaning up an animal facility isn't listed in your job description—"

"Not even remotely," Cole interrupted.

"But I have a plan. And I need you both to hear me out."

They looked at each other before giving me the nod to proceed.

I led them to the conference room where I had laid out my paperwork. "Obviously, we can't do any onsite advertising—television spots, photos, or interviews—at the facility as is. We can't count on Mrs. Teague to fix something she doesn't believe is broken, either, so that leaves it to us."

Ashlyn shifted in her chair. Her being pregnant wasn't ideal for my plan. "Why don't we tell Mr. Hobbs that we can't do it?"

Cole spoke up before I got a chance. "We've been over this, Ash. Hobbs told us we can't afford to lose any more clients."

"I know, I know. I'm just not up to much physical labor in this condition."

"So that's the thing I want to talk about. The way I see it, the animals are well fed, but they need to be exercised and cleaned—actually, the whole place needs a good scrubbing. I think some fresh paint on the signs would help, too. Then there's Mrs. Teague. Ash, you always look pulled together; how would you feel about giving Mrs. Teague a makeover? That is, if I can talk her into it?"

Ashlyn looked at me like I'd broken out in spots.

I waved my hand in front of her face to break her trance. "Just think about it for a while, will you? And Cole, you and I can do the cleaning."

"It sounds like too much for the two of us, Chrissy. Plus, I'm still working on the jingle for the television spot."

"There won't be a television spot if we don't get the place cleaned."

They both looked down at the table. I was sure they were thinking of any other way to make this work. Or possibly how to get me fired.

"I know I'm going out on a limb asking you to do this, but I think we can get it all done in a few Saturdays."

They both groaned so loud I had to cover my ears.

"You can bring your husband, Ash. And, Cole, you can bring your flavor of the week."

He kicked me under the table.

"I need to know you're in before I ask Mr. Hobbs if we can get overtime for working on Saturdays. …C'mon guys." I held my breath. "Okay. I get it. You need to think about it. Just let me know by the end of the day."

Cole left abruptly, but Ashlyn stayed to pelt me with questions.

I answered them as well as I could, but soon realized I needed to spend a lot more time with Mrs. Teague before turning her over to Ashlyn. "I'll find out, Ash. Just say you'll do it if she agrees to all your stipulations."

Ashlyn finally consented. Problem was, her stipulations were many. She wondered if Mrs. Teague would be financing this makeover. And if she would not only let Ashlyn help her with her gaudy makeup, but with her wardrobe, as well. Most important, she asked if I could get Mrs. Teague to bathe before Ashlyn touched her.

Ugh. I thought I had given her the easy job.

I decided to call the woman in question.

"Hello, Mrs. Teague. It's Chrissy Frost. How about another lunch date?"

Maybe Decker had a lovely lady named Breanna to dine with each day, but I had the lovely, crazy-haired, chain-smoking Melba Teague.

****

Decker…I wished I knew how to describe him after last Wednesday. I couldn't, because he was such a mystery. A gorgeous mystery, but still a mystery. If only I could climb into his head and know what he was thinking; he never talked about himself. Sitting next to him today made me sort of wish I were a therapist and had him spill his feelings. I didn't have much time before my appointment, but I had enough to pump him with a few questions I needed answers to like—"Do you have a girlfriend?" I couldn't lead with that one, though.

I looked into those beautiful brown eyes and asked, "How old are you, Decker?" Yeah, I started small.

He blanched at my boldity—haha. *I know that's not a word. Just sounded so right.*

"I'm twenty-six." He fumbled with the papers he'd been looking at before I'd arrived.

Why would that make him nervous? The question wasn't loaded—quite straightforward. Maybe he really was using me as a test subject. If so, I didn't like it. I'd kept men at arm's length. If I trusted him—even as a

45

friend—only to be let down, it would be a hard fall.

"Is this your dream job?"

He inclined his head.

"I mean, will it be your dream job...you know." I hoped he knew. I wasn't certain I knew what I was talking about. I'd only received bits and pieces of things Linda *thought* she'd heard—unreliable, at best. But I needed to learn something about him. After all, I had done all the talking last week; his turn.

"Chrissy, I doubt you want to hear the details of my boring life. But if you really want to know, therapy—helping people—is my dream job...but I need to complete my residency before I can truly feel I have the tools to be a good psychiatrist. Hopefully, I'll be able to get back to that soon."

The temperature in the room dropped, but I pressed on. I needed to know his motivation—interest in me, or pity? I'd cling to one, run from the other.

"What happened? Why the detour?" Now I was being nosy. My mother just rolled over in her grave—Dad, too.

Decker's face did a strange little contortion. I couldn't read what he wasn't about to tell me. But I could sense that something unpleasant had happened to cause the temporary halt to his education.

Chapter Six

"Chrissy." Linda's voice drew my attention away from Decker. *I think I heard him let out a breath. I guess he doesn't want to tell me why he's here instead of somewhere else doing his residency. Or maybe it has to do with that girl, Breanna. Either way, if he can't let me in, I should be more careful about getting too close.*

Linda's eyebrows furrowed. Apparently, she was tired of waiting for me to sort things out in my mind.

"Is Dr. Brandt ready to see me?"

"No. She's at the hospital with a patient. Sorry. She sends her apologies and asked me to tell you she won't be back in time to see you today."

I was a bit disappointed, but now I had more time to grill Decker.

I turned toward him and noticed he was staring a hole through his papers. He really didn't want to talk about himself. It seemed unfair after all the personal information I'd unloaded on him. My heart hurt.

"I guess I'll go." What else could I do? I didn't have a reason to be there any longer. I stood to leave.

Decker's head snapped up as he tugged on my hand. "Wait, Chrissy."

I sat back down and gave him my best you-won't-talk-to-me-so-why-am-I-here? look.

"Last week you mentioned a Mrs. Teague. I've been wondering since then how it's been going."

I shrugged. "Okay. I can tell you about Mrs. Teague."

Decker let out a breath and the worry line creasing his forehead flattened. I didn't know whether to be hurt or flattered. I wished I understood him even a little. Our relationship—if you could call it that—definitely seemed one-sided.

He smiled and looked at me expectantly.

Since my brain had been in a bit of a fog from my panic attack, I couldn't remember everything I had told him concerning Mrs. Teague and the Doggone It facility, but he filled me in so I could continue the story.

"Well, I've had to be creative with our marketing campaign. So creative, in fact, that I've arranged for one of my coworkers to give Mrs. Teague a complete makeover. In the meantime, Cole and I will be giving her facility a complete makeover." I pulled a face and pinched my nose.

"Who's Cole?" His voice sounded unexpectedly flat.

"Oh, Cole is just God's gift to women—his definition, not mine. He and Ashlyn are working with me on this project. He's a decent worker as long as he can't see his reflection." I laughed. "And when there aren't any girls around. I think we're safe with Mrs. Teague." I wondered why he cared about Cole.

"What about you and Ashley, is it?"

"Ashlyn." I emphasized the lyn. "She's married—and pregnant. Cole does have boundaries."

"And you?"

I had just said Cole was super into himself. Hmm. "Well, Cole and I went out for a while, but nothing came of it because I saw him for what he is—shallow."

"And you're still okay working together."

"Yes. Perfectly. Can I finish my story?"

Decker's cheeks turned a charming shade of red. "Sorry. Of course."

"So I took Mrs. Teague out to lunch and laid out my proposal. You can imagine her reaction. She really doesn't know how bad the place looks and smells. She's simply too old to be trying to run a pet facility without more help."

"What about the makeover—hers, I mean?"

"Surprisingly, she acted excited about that. Actually, excited is an understatement. She grabbed both my hands and said, 'Really? You'd do that for me?' " My eyes burned. I had to stop talking and regain my composure.

"Are you all right, Chrissy?" Decker handed me a tissue he'd pulled from a dispenser on the corner table. I wiped my tears and nodded. He patted my arm and left his hand there. Warm and comforting.

"It's just, at lunch that day, I caught a glimpse of the real Mrs. Teague. The woman who needs a friend. She's lonely and wants to be loved—like we all do."

Decker slid his hand down my arm and captured my fingers.

My heart flip-flopped.

"You're a good person, Chrissy." He lifted my hand to his mouth and kissed it.

Wow. Chills.

He glanced at his watch. "It's noon. I've got to run. Can't wait to hear more." He smiled his killer smile. "See you next week?"

I nodded and walked out behind him. Strangely, it

felt as if I'd had a therapy session…with Decker. Now if I could only get him to open up to me, things would be great. I didn't understand why I'd become so drawn to him—especially when he refused to talk about himself. Shouldn't that raise some red flags? But his depth of character and maturity, along with the kindness he'd shown me, were traits I loved and had searched for in a man. He also seemed to understand me. Was that his training, or was he somehow empathetic to my emotional needs? I wished I knew the answers, because my heart was becoming more and more attached to the man.

****

"More breadsticks?"

Mrs. Teague nodded to the waiter.

We were on our third basket. I'd only eaten one stick. After weeks of dining at The Mason Jar, she informed me that she would much prefer eating at The Olive Garden. Now I knew why—bottomless salad and breadsticks.

"Your facility is looking pretty good, don't you think? I figure we'll have it ready to begin promotions after one more Saturday of work. And you…you look amazing." I wasn't lying. Ashlyn had done a remarkable job transforming her.

She gave her hair—which had somehow gained a few pounds—a gentle touch here and there. "I never knew I could look s'good. That gal ya sent over ta fix me up sure knows what she's doin'." She smiled, and I couldn't believe the change. Just a touch of makeup now, perfect for her age. Her teeth were coffee stained, but her smile softened the hard lines of her angular face. The light pink lipstick looked quite pretty.

It had taken some work, but I'd gotten Mrs. Teague to trust me. I still had one question I hadn't dared to ask—why? Why a pet boarding and grooming facility? I needed to know so I could understand her motivation.

I took a slow drink of my soda, then waited for the waiter to finish refilling the breadbasket. "So, Mrs. Teague—"

"Oh, you silly girl. I told you ta call me Melba. Ya make me feel s'old with that missus business."

"I'm sorry. Melba, can I ask you…why do you own a pet facility? I mean, do you enjoy it?"

Blank stare.

Oh no. And it had been going so well.

She looked down, and I could tell she was trying not to cry.

Rats. I figured there would be a strange answer, but I hadn't expected tears.

Finally, she cleared her throat and raised her head. Dabbing at her eyes, she looked from side to side, as if she was going to tell me a secret. "I do it for Jonny."

"Jonny?" My imagination could run in a thousand different directions with that one, but instead I forced my full attention to what she was about to say.

"Yes, Jonathan. He's…er…he was my son." She blew her nose into the napkin.

I said a silent thank you that I'd finished eating.

"He opened the place 'bout five years ago, then last spring he died. Cancer. He was all I had in this world." She began to sob.

My heart ached for her. "So you keep the facility open because he'd want you to?" I placed a hand over Melba's.

She nodded. "I know I'm not doin' a very good job

at runnin' it. I can hardly keep a steady staff and I've heard'em complainin' 'bout me. But I've gotta make it work fer Jonny."

"Do you need the income?"

"Nah. Jonny's life insurance covers all my expenses. I've never been one t'spend a lot a money. Jonny was such a good boy. His father left us flat when he was only eight, and Jonny acted like the man of the family from that day on."

Now I thought I might cry, too. Oh, how I'd misjudged this woman. "Have you considered hiring a manager? That way you wouldn't have to run it, just oversee things."

She looked at me thoughtfully. I hoped she was hearing the wisdom in my words. A manager could be the answer to her problems.

I pressed forward. "It's so much work to take care of animals, as well as the office accounts, and everything. And once Cole, Ashlyn, and I are finished, it would be a shame if you weren't able to keep it looking nice." I rushed to add, "Not that you aren't doing a decent job. I mean, the animals are fed. It's just, they need a good scrubbing and some exercise now and then. And the kennels are hard to keep clean, too."

"I know." She let out a heavy sigh. "The kids I hire seem to come and go as they please. I thought I could do it, but when we started t'lose s'many customers, I figgered I'd better get some help. That's why I called your company."

"If I help you advertise and interview a manager, would you consider hiring? I think Jonny would want that. Plus, I bet he'd hate to see how much work running Doggone It is for you."

"Oh, would ya, honey?" She blew her nose again. The cloth napkin didn't have a dry spot left on it.

I tried to flag the waiter down to get more napkins, but he was nowhere to be found. "Of course, I would. How about I run to the restroom and grab some tissues?"

"Yer so kind, Chrissy. You'd a liked my Jonny."

I didn't know why, but that touched my heart. "I'll be right back." My voice hitched, and I knew I'd better get those tissues quick.

As I wandered through the maze of lunchtime diners, aiming for the restroom, I caught a glimpse of dark blond hair, the same color as Decker's. Wait, the closer I got, the more certain I became—I was looking at the back of Decker's head. He sat way over at a corner table, so I couldn't casually walk by. "And that must be Breanna," I whispered. There she sat— everything I'd imagined and more. Her hair hung in golden waves that framed her perfect face.

Wow. She's gorgeous.

He turned just enough to confirm my suspicion. Decker, no doubt at all. My stomach twisted into a knot.

Chapter Seven

I hated that I cared so much that Decker had a girlfriend. I'd been pretty sure he had someone else in his life all along, but somehow seeing him with her stung. It shouldn't have. I mean, he wasn't my boyfriend. *What is he to me? A friend, I suppose.* I'd hoped for more. And in the theater, I thought we'd had a moment, but I guess there had been no "we" about it. I'd had a moment. He'd just been kind. No wonder he never wanted to talk about himself. It made me feel so…used.

I stared at myself in the restroom mirror. Breanna and I were polar opposites. My long, brunette hair also hung in waves, but they certainly didn't sit as model-perfect as hers. Breanna's had bounced playfully on her petite shoulders while she twinkled her crystal-blue eyes at Decker. Unfortunately—or fortunately, I couldn't decide which—that was all I could see— Breanna's perfect head. But I was sure that a gorgeous body was attached to it. My hazel eyes looked dull brown today. And they didn't twinkle. Which reminded me of the reason I'd gone to the restroom in the first place. Tissues. I plunged my hand into the decorative holder and grabbed a handful, then headed back to Mrs. Teague. I swallowed hard and kept my eyes forward. I couldn't bear to look at Decker and his flawless girlfriend.

Luckily, we were ready to leave. I paid the tab and drove Melba back to Doggone It. She was chatty enough for both of us, thank goodness. My heart hurt, and I didn't feel like talking any more than necessary. She exited the car with a promise of another lunch to plan a strategy for hiring a manager. I'd never seen her so happy. Quite the contrast to my sudden despondency.

****

"Mountainside Medical, this is Kiera. Can I help you?"

A puff of air escaped my lungs. If Linda had answered my call, she'd not let me wiggle out of my appointment. Kiera didn't know me as well.

"Hi, Kiera, this is Chrissy Frost. I'm not going to be able to make my appointment today. Things are crazy at work, and I can't leave." I wasn't really lying. Things were crazy, but after seeing Decker and Miss Perfect at the restaurant yesterday, I couldn't put my heart through possibly seeing him at the clinic.

"Okeydokey. We'll see you next week?"

"Sure." *Unless I can think of another excuse.* "When do you expect Dr. Peterson back, so I can start coming on Tuesdays again?" A question I never thought I'd hear myself ask.

"I don't know. Sorry, Ms. Frost."

I ended the call and dug into the pile on my desk. Hating cold weather meant I put everything into my work during late autumn and winter. And having a broken heart was a definite bonus for Hobbs and Bevins. I'd become a pro at pushing anything hurtful to the very corners of my heart, where I wouldn't have to feel it.

"Chrissy?"

"Uncle Simon. How did you know where I worked?" I jumped to my feet and pulled him into a hug. His luxurious-smelling cologne reminded me of my dad. I swiped at a tear before it could fall.

"I have my ways." He chuckled. "Any chance you could slip away for an early lunch?"

There was every chance I could slip away for lunch, since I'd canceled my counseling appointment. I had tons of work, but I needed to eat. "Your timing is impeccable. I happen to have the next hour open."

"Fabulous." He crooked his arm like a perfect gentleman, and we dashed off to lunch.

It surprised me that he opted to eat at a simple sandwich shop. He had all the trappings of a man-about-town. He wore name-brand clothing and drove a Mercedes. A few years my father's senior, his silvering hair made him look extra distinguished.

Just as I sank my teeth into my turkey sandwich, he said, "You seem to have a good job for such a young girl."

I chewed for a moment before replying. "I think I lucked out. Hobbs and Bevins hired me straight out of college. Somehow, I've convinced them they can't do without me." I lowered my voice, "It's all smoke and mirrors."

Simon let out a hearty laugh. "And a lot of hard work, I'm sure."

His smile helped me forget my troubles for a while.

We talked of work and family. He said he was a consultant. I didn't know who he consulted, but I was sure he was good at it.

"Tell me about this hospital project you and your

sisters are involved in." He popped a chip into his mouth.

I couldn't help but smile. "I'd love to. You see, when my baby brother Nick had so many problems with his heart, my parents spent a lot of time driving to Denver for treatments. Specialists were optimistic he'd have a normal life one day. Just when we thought he'd reached that point, he took a turn for the worse. He was life-flighted to Denver, but...died in transit." I shrugged, remembering the intense sadness our family had experienced after his death. Uncle Simon surely knew about Nicky.

The look on his face said no. But he nodded. "So you're spending the Frost inheritance on a new wing at the hospital?"

This conversation just become oddly personal. "Um, Mom and Dad had earmarked Dad's portion of his inheritance from Grandpa for the wing. They'd started the ball rolling after Grandpa died. Then...well, you know." I had to blink back tears burning my eyes. "We only continued what they had begun. The groundbreaking is November thirtieth. You should come."

He agreed, then looked at his watch. "I guess it's time I got you back to work."

"Thanks for lunch, Uncle Simon. I needed to get out."

****

By Saturday I'd put in close to fifty hours at the office, and now I would put in another five or six at Doggone It. Snow had fallen during the night, blanketing the Springs and chilling my bones. To anyone else, it looked beautiful. To me, it looked deadly. Thank goodness it had stopped falling and now only taunted me from the ground. Gray clouds still hung over the valley, but I had to go to the pet facility. If everything went according to plan, we'd finish up today.

Holly and I had gone shopping a few weeks before at the mall. I'd fallen in love with a super-soft red sweater and had to buy it. Holly said it brought out my rosy cheeks and looked smashing with my dark hair—her words. I didn't use words like smashing. I'd nearly forgotten about it because our office at Hobbs and Bevins was pretty warm—too warm for a cozy sweater like the one I'd bought. Today would be the perfect day to wear it.

I tugged on my snow boots and down parka and headed out the door.

Cole, Ashlyn, and Jared—Ashlyn's husband—pulled into the parking lot at Doggone It right as I did.

Cole leered then winked at me. "Lookin' good, Chrissy."

I scowled in response.

The place had kennels inside and out, plus a wide-open play area that was now white with snow. *It is really kind of nice*, I thought. *It even smells better. I imagine Doggone It had been quite the popular facility to take one's pets, back when Jonny ran it.*

Mrs. Teague only had one groomer on her staff—or so she said. I never saw him—and a couple of employees who worked nights. She needed a few more people to keep up the place. The new manager she'd promised to hire would be a big help.

I sent Ashlyn in with a list of things to explain to Mrs. Teague concerning the television crew due to invade her facility on Monday morning. Ash would also need to rearrange some of the furnishings, so it would show well on film. Her husband Jared was a huge help with the grooming. I didn't know where he'd learned it, but he showed up with his own fur-snipping implements and went straight to work. Cole had spent weeks cleaning the entire inside and still had some work to do. That left me with the kennels and grounds outside. Thankfully, they were canopied so the snow hadn't covered the muck. I grabbed my shovel and went to work.

At noon Mrs. Teague clanged a metal triangle, scaring the jellybeans out of me.

"Lunch time," she hollered.

I giggled. She really was a funny lady.

Everyone stopped what they were doing and gathered around her kitchenette to eat chili and homemade bread. Thank goodness she'd maintained her living quarters better than the animal facility.

"This is delicious." A mouthful of fluffy bread melted on my tongue as I spoke. My mother would be scolding me if she were here. She had been all about manners.

Mrs. Teague walked around the table with the chili pot, asking everyone if they wanted seconds. When she reached me, she put it down and gave me an unexpected hug. "You made this all happen," she whispered in my ear. "I can't thank you enough." A tear leaked from the corner of her eye. "I'm just sa sorry it's all gonna be over soon. I've loved havin' ya here, and I've espeshly enjoyed our lunches t'gether."

A lump formed in my throat. I couldn't believe this was the same woman I'd met only a few weeks before.

"What do you think about this, Mrs....Melba?" She smiled when I used her first name. It felt awkward to me, but she'd kept insisting. "How about you and I keep going out to lunch once a week?"

I thought we might both tip over when she clapped her arms around me and kissed my cheek. "Yes. I think that's a mighty fine idea."

Now I had leaky eyes, and I realized what this kind lady had done for me. She'd begun to fill an empty place in my heart that had once belonged to my mother. Was I willing to let her occupy that sacred space? My heart warmed in reply to my thoughts. I guess time would tell, but for now I liked the feeling.

Once lunch was cleaned up, Ashlyn, Jared, and Cole packed their belongings and headed home.

I still had a few kennels to muck. The dark clouds nearly touched the ground, so I hurried outside. I dreaded the approaching storm.

I moved vigorously, shedding my parka, which had become an impediment. I could feel it in my bones—the snow was coming. Fixing my sights on cleaning the kennels, I barely heard the gate creak open. Snow-muffled footsteps brought my head up, but before I could turn to see who was there, a familiar voice made my heart skip a beat.

"Chrissy?"

I spun around. I couldn't believe it or mistake it. Deliciously perfect, velvety smooth-voiced Decker was there. And then I remembered—and taken. Ugh. I stood with my mouth gaping open.

He smiled and held up a shovel. "Thought you could use some help."

"But how? Why?"

"Well, the how is easy. You texted me about coming here on Saturdays a while back, and the why…" He pushed the gate open and pointed at the sky, which had been hidden from my view by the kennel's tin awnings. Snowflakes the size of the Grand Canyon tumbled in circles before touching down.

I stiffened.

He captured my eyes with those piercing brown ones of his, scoping out fires that might be about to explode inside me. I blinked back tears.

"I'm here to help. Would you like to go home, and I'll finish?" His voice was gentle and reassuring.

I shook my head. "No. I need to be here to make sure we've done everything. Television crews arrive Monday. I can't leave until I know Mrs. Teague is ready."

"Then I'll help." He began to shovel.

I stared at him in disbelief. Nobody else I knew, besides my sisters, would ever show up to make sure I was all right just because snow fell from the sky—no one.

"Thank you." I didn't know what else to say.

He smiled and began to hum *Jingle Bells*.

I cringed. Snow and Christmas carols—two of my least favorite things. Winter brought death and sorrow.

He watched my reaction out of the corner of his eye and stopped and frowned. "Does Christmas music bother you?"

"Yes. All of it," I snapped. "I'll bet it doesn't bother cute little Breanna," I muttered under my breath.

"What?"

"Nothing." I plunged my shovel into the muck. *He shouldn't be here, messing with my head and my heart.*

61

"Don't you think it's time to let go of those feelings? Christmas didn't kill your parents."

I froze. He was right. I'd never thought of it that way. I didn't know why I continued to let the season control me. I gawked at him, realizing he had shaken some sense into me.

"But snow—" Splat! A snowball hit me on the arm. "Snow is definitely evil." He winked.

My eyes nearly popped out of my head. He had really thrown a snowball at me. I looked around for my parka and saw I'd left it several kennels over.

Decker had moved to the dogs' play area.

I decided against retrieving my coat before gathering ammo. No one threw a snowball at me and got away with it. My sisters had learned that the hard way—long ago. I scooped up some handfuls of snow and began forming balls. Another one hit my back. Oh man, he was asking for it. Before snow had, had a paralyzing effect on me, I'd been the snowball fight queen. Another one whistled through the air, but I dodged it and ducked behind a wheelbarrow upturned by the fence. I filled it with my perfect, round balls and started to fire away. One landed squarely on his smugly handsome face.

He didn't back down. "Thought you were afraid of snow," he yelled before lobbing a huge clump at me.

"I thought you were here to protect me from it," I yelled back, shooting off three in a row. Snow clung to his hair. "And if you're going to start a fight, you should wear a hat." I tried to act mad, but I couldn't help but smile at the sight of him. Soon, though, the snow seeped into my sweater, and my teeth chattered.

"I was trying to fight fair; after all, you're not

wearing a coat and you're freezing."

Freezing or not, the snowballs kept coming. He was moving closer, but I was determined to outlast him.

Gathering up all my ammo, I ran straight into him, shoving snow into his chest and face.

He fell backward, and I came down on top of him. I tried to prop myself up, but he pulled me back into his embrace. As I was shivering, he rubbed my back. I was sure he was trying to massage some warmth into me. It worked. My heart thudded at a rapid pace, and every nerve in my body tingled. He loosened his grip enough for me to look at him. I wanted to cry.

You might think you're playing fair, but this is not fair.

In one smooth motion, he lifted me off and sat up, pulling me with him. His arm remained around my waist, our faces inches apart. Those eyes that were always watching out for me locked with mine.

"I missed you on Wednesday."

Before I had a chance to respond to his caramelness, his warm lips were on mine. Okay, never mind. There simply was no response for that. I didn't resist. I let my arms slide around his neck. I'd never felt so safe in my life. I didn't know what was happening.

When the lusciously long, but not long enough, kiss ended, I collected my wits, which were strewn all around the kennel.

"Decker? But what about—"

"I've wanted to do that since the first day I met you." The words vibrated against my willing lips, shaking the earth, or at least my heart.

Never mind the snow, Melba, or Bre…what's-her-name.

I went in for more delicious kisses from the gorgeous man holding me.

Chapter Eight

"That's what I'm saying, Elle—he kissed me!"

I don't know why I chose to call Noelle. Well, that's not true. She and I had some kind of weird connection when it came to guys. I think she saw me as "safe" with her secrets because of our age difference. And she'd told me a few. I guess I trusted her, as well.

I'd stretched out on the sofa, wrapped up in a velvety blanket. A vanilla candle emitted a soothing fragrance. I watched as the flame danced. My roommate had left town and wouldn't be back until after Thanksgiving—some people actually liked the holidays instead of dreading them. I was glad she was gone so I could be lazy. Her OCD-ness kept me perpetually on my toes. Today I only wanted to figure out the conflict happening in my brain.

"You can't be kissing your therapist, Chrissy. You can't be kissing your therapist." She used her big-sister-knows-best voice.

"Eww, yuck. I didn't kiss my therapist. I said I met him at the therapist's office. They're very different things."

She let out a breath. "So you didn't kiss Dr. Peterson?"

"Oh my gosh, Elle. Are you even listening to me? Why would I kiss Dr. Peterson? He's old. I think I'm going to be sick."

"Sorry. Okay, so you met some guy at the clinic and kissed him in the snow."

Now *I* let out the frustrated breath. "Close enough."

"What happened after that?"

"I don't know. I mean, he hugged me for a long time, because I was wet and freezing. But then we finished our work. I think we both felt a little awkward. It's all a blur because I swear I was in shock." *And on cloud 999.* "I don't know what to make of it. Last week I saw him out with another girl, and—"

"Oh no." Elle cut me off.

I knew red flags were waving, lights flashing, and sirens blaring for her. She'd been through the worst kind of "other woman" experience.

"Elle, I don't think he's like that. He's the kindest man I've ever met. I just need to figure things out in my mind. Please don't jump to conclusions before I have more information."

"Chrissy, I thought all the same things about Blake. You can't be too careful. So many men are—"

"Okay." I interrupted. "Well, I've got to go." *And maybe call Joy or Holly. Geez.* I'd picked the wrong sister this time.

I spent a lot of time that Sunday puzzling out what had happened the day before. Decker surely had feelings for me, right? I thought he'd started the snowball fight to force me to face my fears. It worked, but I also ended up face-to-face with him. Was that planned? If so, I didn't like it. My heart was too wrapped up in the guy. I was falling in love, but I had no idea if he had real feelings for me. He'd given me hints that he did—lots of them. But then I didn't know why he always clammed up when conversation about him became personal. Share and share alike, my mom always said. And...what about Breanna? I pulled a pillow over my face and groaned.

My phone interrupted me. Joy's face flashed on my screen. *Oh, no. I hope Elle didn't go straight to Joy and spill.* I took a breath before I answered. "Hey, Joy. What's up?"

"How's your Sunday going?" Whew. She didn't have that motherly I-heard-what-you're-up-to voice.

"Good. And yours?" I knew she relished her time with her three adorable boys—especially on the weekends.

"Great. Just got home from church. We need to plan Thanksgiving. I know we talked about this at dinner last Friday night, but I need to double check. Do you still want to bring the usual?"

We held all our family gatherings at Joy's house in the Peregrine area of town. Not only was the home spacious and beautiful, but it was where we spent our childhood. When our parents died, the house was left to the four of us. Not wanting to part with so many wonderful memories, we'd all thought Joy and Tom had a great idea when they'd offered to buy Elle, Holly, and me out. They moved in and did some awesome remodeling, which was Joy's passion. Not so much renovating, though, that it took away from what my parents had done. I loved that house.

"If by the usual you mean sweet potatoes and the relish dish, then, yes," I said. An idea nearly knocked me over. "Hey, do you think it would be all right if I bring a friend?"

"Like a boyfriend? Is there something you haven't

told me, Chrissy?"

I did my best to guffaw. "No, not a boyfriend. I want to bring Melba Teague. The woman I told you about from the Doggone It Boarding and Grooming Facility. I think she's alone for the holidays. It would be nice for her to have somewhere to go." I hated the thought of Melba sitting at her dinette, eating alone.

"Do you think she can handle our...well, our craziness?"

I knew what she meant. Thanksgiving officially kicked off the holidays, and we always spent it together—kind of a family therapy session where we buoyed each other up to face the stormy weeks ahead.

"I think she's had her share of craziness, too. It's got to be better than spending Thanksgiving with a bunch of howling animals—she lives right next to the kennels."

"Then absolutely. We will welcome her with open arms."

I knew I could count on Joy. Her heart was twice the size of anyone else's.

****

I awoke early Monday morning with two things—a text and the jitters. The text was from Decker, telling me what a nice time he'd had on Saturday. The jitters were a result of the day's upcoming project. I wanted to focus on the text but couldn't because of the anxiety pulsing through my veins.

Filming a commercial at Doggone It was on the docket, and I'd had a nightmare about arriving and finding the place a mess—the way it had been before we'd all pitched in to spiff it up. I wanted to get there first so I could see for myself that all was well. Plus, I worried about Melba. This might be invasive for her. But I reminded myself she'd asked for it. *And now I feel protective of her.* I smiled, thinking of the wonderful person I'd discovered in the strangest place—a run-down pet facility.

I shot off a response to Decker saying I appreciated his help and enjoyed his company. Then I texted my work team and told them I would meet them at the facility.

When I arrived, I breathed a grateful sigh of relief. The place still looked pristine, probably thanks to Kevin, the new manager my team had helped to hire. Melba wore her assigned outfit and she'd obediently held off on her hair and makeup. Ashlyn would take care of that. I gave her a hug. I could tell she was as nervous as I was.

"If all goes well, we should be able to get what we need today and be done with the filming." I tried to calm her. "For sure by tomorrow." I crossed my fingers. "Do you want to rehearse your lines with me?"

She did.

We spent the next fifteen minutes going over her lines, which were very few—we didn't want her backwoods twang to be on display. It helped us both feel a little more prepared.

Eventually, the rest of the gang showed up, including the family of actors we'd hired for the commercial.

"Oh, and, Melba, before I forget, and it gets too hectic around here, would you like to join me and my sisters for Thanksgiving dinner?"

That may have been a mistake. She wrapped me in the biggest bear hug ever. Marble-sized tears rolled off her face. I motioned to Ashlyn, who had just done Melba's makeup, to bring her touch-up kit.

Between sobs, she managed a few words. "Well, ain't you the kindist thing?" She blew her nose. "Since Jonny died, I've spent my special days, like my birthday, alone. This'll be my first Thanksgivin' without'im." More tears. "I'm sa sorry to mess up m'makeup."

When I looked at Ashlyn, expecting to see angry darts aimed at me, I was surprised to see her eyes brimming with tears. That was all it took for me to lose it.

I grabbed a handful of tissues from the box Melba held. "Aren't we a bunch of watering pots?" I gathered them both into a group hug.

The filming went well except for a few glitches. Several times the dogs howled so loudly we couldn't hear the actors. And my personal favorite—an hour of footage disappeared when the camera, inadvertently left running, captured Cole taking a personal call—a very personal call. I tried not to overhear, but I thought someone was breaking up with him. There may have been some tears. Cole crying was not pretty. I couldn't imagine where that footage went.

I'd learned to expect glitches—they were part of the job. I thought Melba was secretly happy that we'd have to return on Tuesday to finish up with things. I was, too.

My phone buzzed Tuesday morning. Mountainside Medical Clinic. I'd hardly had a chance to think about my therapy sessions with everything going on at Doggone It. My shoulder and neck muscles hardened into tight knots. "Hello?"

"Hi, Chrissy. It's Linda at Mountainside. Just a reminder that we are canceling all appointments for the rest of the week."

The knots began to untangle. "Okay, thanks, Linda. I'll see you next week, then." I meant it. It was time I grew up and stuck with my therapy until I no longer needed it—no matter who I might run into.

"Sounds good. Have a nice holiday." Linda gave her signature laugh at the end of her sentence.

I was surprised the word "holiday" didn't cause me some internal trauma, as it had in the past. Maybe Dr. Brandt had tapped into some of my darkness and shooed it away. And Decker had definitely helped.

I knew he had nothing to do with my therapy sessions, but somehow—probably because we'd met at the clinic—I'd begun to associate the two. He made me feel I was worth loving. Dr. Brandt had said the words, but Decker made them true.

I wondered where he'd be spending Thanksgiving. Probably in Chicago with his family. I sighed.

****

Thanksgiving was amazing. Everyone extended a warm welcome to Melba—I was finally getting used to calling her that now. We sat around Joy's large table, which had been my parents' before, and I couldn't help but think some kind of magic shimmered in the air. Of course, magic sizzled on the table. Thanksgiving dinner was the best. Joy knew how to roast a turkey—one whiff and my mouth salivated—and I knew how to make the yummiest sweet potato casserole around. I swore I could eat the whole bowl of it by myself. But I didn't. I knew there were at least five million calories per serving. Holly brought mashed potatoes and her famous green bean casserole, and Elle—well, she was the queen of baking. She brought rolls and ten pies. Yum. The little ones were on their best behavior. Perfect. Of course, it didn't hurt that I slipped Charlie, Tatum, and the twins candy when no one was looking. It was important to keep my favorite-aunt status. I wasn't above bribery.

I'd decided I'd only remember Decker's kisses and forget all of my insecurities—for today. And looking at each of my sisters, who appeared a bit rosier than usual, made me think perhaps they'd had a few kisses of their own they were reflecting on. I hoped so. Joy for sure had. She'd invited a handsome man and his little boy. The looks they traded were hard to miss.

Someone was missing, however. "Joy, I thought you invited Uncle Simon. Where is he?"

Elle and Holly exchanged a glance I couldn't decipher.

Joy cleared her throat, bringing my attention back to her. "I invited him, but he said he had business out of town."

"On Thanksgiving?" I shrugged and took a bite of turkey. "His loss, I suppose."

"Uncle Simon is proving to be quite a mysterious man." Joy poured gravy over her potatoes. She then shocked us with an announcement that Uncle Simon had donated a sizeable amount of money to the Frost Foundation. I wasn't surprised. If he was anything like Dad, he was all about helping others.

Amid the conversation and stuffing my face, I almost didn't hear my phone chime. "That's strange. Who would be texting me?" I shouldn't have said that aloud. Now I had everyone's attention.

"Who is it, Chrissy?" Elle looked at me with arched eyebrows.

Decker. And, no, I didn't want to share. "It's nobody, Elle."

"Well, that means it's definitely somebody." She reached for my phone.

I jumped up and held it away from her. "Ahem, if we're going to go there, Elle, then I might as well mention a tree—the tall variety." I fled the room before she could strangle me. I'd done so well keeping her crush a secret, but she knew I'd tell if she breathed one word about Decker.

I hid in the bathroom to read the text. I didn't know why; it would probably only say "Happy Thanksgiving." I just wanted to read it without everyone's eyes on me. I pulled it up and discovered a whole paragraph.

—*Chrissy, snow is coming down pretty hard here in Chicago. It made me think of you. How are you holding up? I know holidays are rough. Wish I could be there. My thoughts are with you.*—

His text touched me. Maybe because I'd expected some trite holiday greeting and instead received a heartfelt message hinting that he cared. "I wonder how I should respond. Hmm." I sat on the edge of the bathtub, staring at three ninja-decorated towels dangling from hooks. *I hope I have some kiddos someday to buy cute towels for,* I thought. Well, that wasn't helpful. I shifted to face a new direction, then began to punch out a reply.

—*Decker, thanks for your concern. It means a lot to me. I'm doing well; I'm with my sisters. We muddle through together. You need to stop worrying about me and enjoy your vacation. Happy turkey day.*—

My phone dinged almost immediately. *—Not worrying so much as I just can't get you off my mind. I'll let you get back to your family.—*

There may have been magic at the dinner table, but this bathroom had just become enchanted. I wanted to float out on my cloud 999 and tell everyone that I was in love with Decker and would be getting married and having little Deckers very soon. I looked in the mirror and shook my head. *Silly me. That's so impractical.* I meant, I was reading an enormous amount into a simple text. And I still had the Breanna problem… But it sure felt good to pretend Decker shared my feelings.

I considered a reply. I hated those kinds of decisions. No. I decided I'd let it end there—on a very good note.

Chapter Nine

In spite of the November chill and the freezing wind, the clouds parted, and the sun sprinkled down rays of warmth. The big day had arrived—the groundbreaking ceremony. We sat on the front row and my stomach fluttered with anticipation. Hospital Chairman of the Board Olivia Winn stepped to the podium to address the crowd. She gave a short, but touching speech.

I leaned over to Joy. "I'm so happy, happier than I believed I could be."

She smiled and blinked back a few tears.

Ms. Winn then invited us to come forward. Hand in hand we headed to the front and took our shovels. Tatum, Charlie, and the twins joined us. I glanced at each sister and saw happy tears in their eyes. The moment was perfect.

My sisters and I had cherished the time we'd spent finishing what our parents had begun. Mom and Dad had lined up donors to match the money they'd put in the Frost Foundation to build the hospital wing, but after they died, many donors had pulled out. It took a lot of convincing on our part to prove to them that we were serious about the project. A quick look at the audience nearly brought on fresh tears. From the front row Richard Arnett, our lawyer, who had helped us every step of the way, beamed at me. And Uncle

Simon, sitting in the back, winked. The more I'd thought about his generous donation to our foundation, the more I loved him. What a decent guy he'd turned out to be. Best of all, I knew my parents were there in spirit.

Right before our shovels hit the frozen earth, a man broke through the line, nearly knocking Charlie over.

I glanced at Holly for reassurance. She shrugged. Elle and Joy looked baffled as well.

"Excuse me, let me through, please." The tall, bald man stepped around to face us. "Mrs. Joy Frost Burton?"

Joy raised her hand. "Yes?"

"And Ms. Noelle Frost, Ms. Holly Frost, and Ms. Christina Frost?" He motioned to the three of us.

We nodded.

What was going on? I looked to Joy for reassurance. Her expression, as blank as the rest of my sisters', didn't give me any comfort.

He handed Joy a packet of papers. "You are officially served."

Joy opened her mouth. "No—"

She was cut off by the bald man. "Have a good day." He pivoted and walked away.

I gasped. "Oh no." Blood drained from my face and my knees wobbled like soggy noodles. The wind picked up and nearly knocked me over. How could this happen? We'd worked so hard attending to every detail.

Joy stood frozen, and the man was gone before we could ask questions. We gathered around her, but my teeth were chattering so hard from the fierce wind slapping me in the face that I couldn't hear what was being said.

Richard Arnett spoke to Joy, and I watched her face pale.

My thoughts in a whirl, I stood in place until he turned to the rest of us. "Ladies, please meet me at my office ASAP." He then turned and said something, dismissing the audience, but I couldn't say what. I clutched Holly's arm for support.

The silent drive to Mr. Arnett's firm seemed endless. Holly and I rode together, and I think we were too stunned to speak.

"What it comes down to, ladies, is the Frost Foundation's assets have been frozen." Mr. Arnett adjusted his glasses. "Have you heard of Lyonstone, LLC?"

All four of us shook our heads.

"Neither have I," he continued. "Lyonstone is claiming a share of the Frost Foundation's money. I'm afraid until we can work through this, construction on the new hospital wing will be delayed."

I sat motionless, certain this nightmare was not happening.

He said he'd work on unraveling the mystery. The words just buzzed around in my head. How could this be? Our family trust fund should have been safe from any outside influence.

Before leaving, Joy asked about the time frame for getting the mess untangled.

"I'm afraid this may take quite some time." He shook his head. "I'm so sorry."

Richard Arnett was as good as they get. He'd worked with our parents for years before their deaths, and with the four of us ever since.

Crying, we huddled together in a group hug. Then

tried to figure a way out of the mess we'd been thrust into. Many suggestions were made, but without knowing how in the world our funds had become frozen, and who was behind it, nothing panned out. In the end, we all trusted Mr. Arnett to get to the bottom of it; however, we soon realized it likely wouldn't happen before the new year. Disappointing.

****

"What is it, Cole?"

After a long weekend of rollercoaster emotions, I didn't want drama at work. We just needed to finish the Doggone It Campaign before Christmas. Not easy when Cole seemed especially needy at our meeting.

"It's the jingle. I've got jingle block."

I let go of a frustrated breath. "Did you come up with that one all by yourself? No wonder you can't write a simple lyric."

"Come on, Chrissy. Will you at least take a look at it and see if you can tell what's missing?" He batted his long, black lashes at me.

I had to look away so I wouldn't give him the satisfaction of seeing me laugh at his pathetic cry for help. "Fine. Let's go into the conference room." We wove through the desks and started down the hall.

Ashlyn stood there, blocking our way. Her round eyes looked like blue saucers on her pale face. Her mouth gaped open in a perfect circle.

"Ash, what's wrong?"

She remained motionless—rooted in place.

I put my hand on her arm. "Ashlyn?"

Those large eyes turned downward. I followed their path to a small puddle on the floor beneath her.

"Uh oh," I said.

"Uh oh what?" asked Cole, ever the clueless one.

"Her water broke, Einstein. We have to get her to the hospital."

"What about my jingle?"

Ashlyn and I both skewered him with deadly glares.

"It's too early. I'm not due for another month," Ashlyn said. Her eyes misted.

No wonder she'd looked terrified. "The sooner we get you to the ER, the better. Cole, call 911."

For once he didn't question me. We could have driven her, but by the pained look on her face and the fact she was delivering so prematurely, I thought she might need a medical professional sooner.

I grabbed Ashlyn's phone and found Jared's number. Her husband needed to be with her. No answer. "Ash, do you know where Jared is?"

Cole pulled a chair over to her, and we made her sit.

"He's at work. If he's in a meeting, he can't answer the phone. Text him."

I punched in a text, hoping he could read the urgency in my words.

The paramedics arrived in ten minutes, causing quite a scene at Hobbs and Bevins. Ashlyn looked scared to death.

Two of them—a man and a woman—helped her lie down on a gurney.

Ashlyn grabbed my arm, her eyes huge. "Will you ride with me, Chrissy?"

"Go ahead, Chrissy," I heard Mr. Hobbs say. His voice far less crusty than usual.

"Okay," I barely whispered. Not that I didn't want

to go with Ashlyn. I did. But an ambulance only went to one place—the hospital. And people died there.

If falling snow gave me anxiety, hospitals put me into apoplectic seizures. Okay, another exaggeration, but I really did hate hospitals. My father had died on the scene of their terrible accident, but my mom had lived long enough to give me some hope. She took her last breath in the hospital two hours later.

Ever since that day, I'd not been able to go into a hospital. I tried when Joy gave birth to the twins Micah and Mitchell. But the minute I'd entered the lobby, those smells—sterility, disease, death, sorrow—assaulted me. The only memory I had was waking up on a sofa at Elle's house, her little Tatum patting my head and saying, "Kissy, Kissy." She was only two, and I'd never forget those sweet, chubby hands on my face. I didn't know if I'd fainted or zoned out. I understood the irony of the Frost Foundation building being something I'd never want to enter, but there it was. I'd observe from a distance.

I divided my time in the ambulance between telling Ashlyn everything would be fine, praying that I wasn't lying, and repeatedly calling and texting Jared. Where was he? If he didn't get to the hospital soon, I'd have to stay, and I really, really needed to leave.

Finally, he answered.

"Jared, Ashlyn's in labor—"

"I got your texts." He sounded out of breath. "I had a conference in Denver."

No. This couldn't be happening.

"I'm on the road, but it will be another thirty minutes before I can get there. Promise me you'll stay with her, Chrissy."

I wanted to sob out loud. I couldn't promise such a thing. Nervous jitters hit me hard. In my head I screamed *no* at the very moment I said, "Of course I will."

I looked down at Ashlyn. She'd overheard our conversation—at least my end of it.

"He's in Denver, isn't he? I forgot about that conference." A tear dripped down the side of her face and wet her hair.

"Is there anybody else you want me to call, Ash? You know I won't leave you, but do you have any family here in the Springs?" *Please say yes, please say yes.*

"No. My parents live in Austin. They moved there a year ago. My brother...well, I don't know where he is."

"I'll call your parents. Even if they can't be here, they'll want to know."

Another tear leaked out of her eye. I found a tissue in my purse and gave it to her. My hand shook, but she didn't seem to notice.

As soon as we arrived at the hospital, they whisked her away. Maybe I could just disappear. "No, I promised Jared." I had to stay. I ran to catch them.

Gosh, by the speed the medics moved, you'd think Ashlyn was having a heart attack instead of a baby. Yes, she was delivering early, but surely no reason for everyone to be in such a panic. I realized that I hadn't listened to any of the paramedic chatter during the ambulance ride. I'd been too preoccupied. Maybe this was more urgent than I'd thought.

Then, without warning I began to gag, the hospital smell choking me.

"Women." The sign on the door couldn't have appeared at a better time. I detoured into the ladies' room, threw the stall door open, and puked in the toilet. Tears blurred my vision. I couldn't do this. I vomited again and again, until I had nothing left in me. I washed my face and let the cool water carry away my tears. My reflection in the mirror was no comfort. Whatever makeup I'd worn was gone. My face was white as a sheet. I bit my lip to stop the incessant teeth chattering. "How can I be there for Ashlyn?" I shook my head and took several deep breaths. "I don't know, but it's time I get over myself and think of her instead of me." I sent a little prayer heavenward for Ashlyn, her baby—and me.

I stepped out of the restroom and asked a nurse where they'd rushed her off to.

"Take the elevator to the fourth floor, then make a right. Ask for her room number at the nurse's station."

I could hear the words, but they danced around in my head, making no sense at all. Yet somehow I stumbled into Ashlyn's room in time to hear "...Eclampsia...mother and child are at risk."

"No." I must have shrieked it out loud because several heads swiveled in my direction.

"Miss, you can't be in here. Are you a relative?"

"Yes...I mean, no. But I promised..."

The door swung open and Jared nearly knocked me over. I let out a huge puff of air.

"It's okay, Chrissy. You can go now."

I should go now. Now that my friend and her baby could die, I should leave. People die during the holidays. My thoughts screamed at me and everyone around me. Thank goodness they were only thoughts.

A kind nurse led me out of the room to a sitting

area. I thought she had to because I'd forgotten how to move. I sank down on a sofa, pulled my knees up to my chest, buried my head in my arms, and cried. I didn't know how long I sat there. Time had become irrelevant the minute I'd entered the hospital. Nausea churned in my stomach. I needed to find another restroom, and fast.

I stood up on wobbly legs and walked aimlessly through the maternity ward. Surely there would be a public restroom nearby. A door opened, and I heard a voice.

"Decker, don't leave."

I hopped out of the way, catching partial sight of the patient's name on the opening door. Breanna.

"I'm getting you some ice chips," the caramel-smooth, traitorous voice replied.

"Chrissy?"

I realized I had stopped and he'd nearly smacked right into me. I gawked at him. Breanna was real. I knew that. I'd seen her with my own eyes. But in my heart of hearts I'd believed in Decker. Believed his kisses meant something; that his words of comfort were more than mere words. That perhaps Breanna had been an associate, a friend from college—anything but a girlfriend. But a baby? This changed everything.

"What are you doing here?" He regarded me oddly.

My eyes were swollen, and my makeup had been scrubbed off. I was sure I looked a mess. Bile rose in my throat. I needed to retch. I clapped a hand over my mouth, willing it away.

Decker's brows furrowed, and he tried to pull me into his arms. "What is it? What happened?"

He obviously had a wife or a girlfriend in labor in

the room just inches away, and he wanted to know what bothered me?

I resisted his embrace. "You…you're…I thought you…I—" Enough. I pushed him away and ran. I had to flee the hospital of death and disappointment. I hadn't forgotten Ashlyn and her baby. I kept a continuous prayer in my heart for her, but right now the deep gash in my soul came from the man I'd begun to love.

"Chrissy."

I heard his voice, but I didn't turn back.

And he didn't chase me.

Of course he didn't, he was having a baby.

Chapter Ten

My car wasn't at the hospital. I could have called Cole to pick me up, but I'd be worthless trying to focus on work in the state I was in. My sisters would all be at their jobs—except Joy, who'd be taking care of her kids. I knew any one of them would drop everything and come, but I didn't feel like explaining myself—especially to Elle. On Thanksgiving she'd pulled me aside to give me a lecture about Decker and how she was sure he had other girlfriends. Maybe she was right. I couldn't tell her that today. Right now, I needed someone to give me unconditional love, the way my mother used to.

"Hello, Melba? I'm in the parking lot at Penrose Hospital. Can you come get me?" I hiccupped from crying so hard.

"Of course I can, sweetie."

Ten minutes later she pulled up in her blue sedan. She jumped out and had me in her arms in seconds.

My tears began again.

We didn't speak at first. She seemed to sense I wanted to be with her and not talk about what had gotten me there. My phone chirped. I looked at it. Six texts. All from Decker. My stomach hurt all over again. I turned it off.

She drove to her home—an extension of her pet facility. I closed my eyes, thinking of the work that remained on her marketing campaign. I had to shove it away.

"Come in, sweetie. I'll make you some hot soup."

Soup. Yes, soup. That's what my mother would've made me on a day like today. I feared anything else she would have suggested might have sent me straight to the bathroom.

She sat me down on a fluffy, camel-colored recliner. It wrapped around me like I was sitting in a hug. "I can have chicken and dumplins ready in justa jiff. Do ya wanna tell me what's gotcha so torn up?"

Did I? My good friend and her baby were at risk of dying. And if that wasn't enough, the man I'd begun to give my heart to was helping his girlfriend—or wife—deliver their baby. My heart hurt so bad, it seemed it had shattered. Maybe telling Melba would help. She felt safe. That must be why I had called her.

I started from the beginning, not leaving anything out.

"Yer parents both died in a car accident?"

I nodded and went on 'til I got to Decker.

"Was he the one you was kissin' in the snow a couple weeks ago?"

Oh gosh, she'd seen that. My face grew hot.

"He's even more fetchin' than Cole. You two will make pretty babies."

My jaw dropped. How ironic. Decker was at the hospital right now with his and Breanna's "pretty baby." Had Melba missed that part, or had I skipped it? Probably skipped it, wishing it weren't true.

"No, we won't. He's taken. I didn't know it then, but I know it now, and I don't plan to ever see that man again."

She looked confused and embarrassed to have brought on such an outburst.

"I'm sorry, Melba." I went on to explain what had happened.

She forced me to scoot over, then wedged herself into the oversized chair beside me and wrapped a comforting arm around my shoulders. She didn't say a word, just held me as I blubbered.

We sat cuddled up like that until we heard the soup boil, splashing droplets onto the hot burner, then sizzling.

"I'll get that, hon." She pulled a plaid blanket from somewhere and put it over my lap.

****

Ashlyn and her baby girl had come through the eclampsia and premature birth unscathed. That was good news. The bad news was now only Cole and I were left working on the Doggone It project. I knew Mrs. Teague would give us an extension, but I wanted it done so I could disappear over the holidays.

I worked harder the next couple of weeks than I ever had before. I thought Mr. Hobbs assigned me as lead on so many projects because he knew I worked best when I needed an escape—which happened often.

Between my aching heart and the abrupt halt to our hospital wing project, I needed a break from reality. My sisters and I were doing what we could to investigate the mystery of the frozen funds—mostly Elle, since she had a nose for investigative news—but, so far, we'd come up frustrated and empty. I didn't know what could have happened to have caused such a thing. It hurt, especially right now—this close to my parents' deaths.

I thought I'd come so far. The snow, the Christmas music, the holiday season in general, had stopped striking fear in my soul. I could thank Decker for that. I could also thank him for my broken heart. I'd quit going to my counseling sessions. I didn't even call—just never went. I couldn't chance running into him there.

I was stronger. I recognized that. But the pain in my heart persisted, and I didn't want to share that with anyone—not even Dr. Brandt.

Decker's texts had eventually slowed down. As time passed, guilt pinched at me for never giving him a chance to explain. So he had a family—I should be happy for him. The thought made me simultaneously ache for the loss and feel childish for my immature reaction. I vowed to read the next text he sent—should there be another.

My bed beckoned me at the end of the long day of work. I nearly climbed in when my phone chirped. Decker. Should I keep the vow I'd just made to myself? I took a deep breath, then read the text.

—*Chrissy, I doubt you're reading my texts, but I am determined to help you. Whatever you were facing at the hospital obviously haunted you. I'm fairly certain it had something to do with your parents' deaths. I have trained for the past several years to counsel patients for circumstances such as yours. Let me help.*—

"That egotistical jerk." I nearly threw my phone across my bedroom. He *was* one of them. I'd been a guinea pig all along—not a girlfriend. Probably not even a friend. No wonder he'd never talked about himself—psychiatrists never shared their own stories. I didn't know why he'd kissed me—probably so I'd resume my counseling and he could continue practicing therapy on me. Used, used, used. He'd used me in the worst way at my most vulnerable time. Surely a "professional" like him could see how devastating his actions had been.

I replied:—*That's all I've been to you—someone to practice your counseling on? Don't bother me again. I'm not your patient.—*

I made a new vow—delete Decker from my phone and from my life. Elle had been right all along. As usual.

****

Weeks passed. I focused solely on work, which wasn't difficult. I still had plenty to do before activating the Doggone It promotion. I dreaded weekends now, without the extra work at the kennels to fill my time. Nevertheless, they arrived at the end of each long week.

The day was Saturday, somewhere in mid-Death-cember. The death of my parents and the death of my happiness. I needed some air. Snow twinkled on the ground beneath blue skies and the winter sun. Okay, I could finally admit that snow was pretty. It crunched under my boots as I walked out to the community mailboxes. Next week I would be celebrating my twenty-fourth birthday. Even though they didn't include personal notes, I still liked to open the free-meal-on-your-birthday cards. I gathered the envelopes and trudged through the snow back to my apartment—careful to knock all the clumps off my boots before entering.

I dumped the mail onto the table and began to sort the junk—which it mostly was. A letter with my name hand-written on it jumped out at me. Nobody wrote letters anymore. Without a second thought, I ripped it open. The letter was lengthy—several pages. I flipped to the end to see—

"Decker."

I didn't know if I should read it or toss it. My thoughts reeled.

"If you don't read it, I will." Kassie startled me. I forgot she'd been in the other room and had evidently entered during my debate.

"How did you know what I was thinking?"

I'd told her all about the Decker situation, once my heart had become strong enough to divulge it to someone other than Melba. Now Kassie had become an ally, as well.

"You nearly stared a hole through it. I figured you were deciding whether to read it or not."

"Fine. I'll read it."

"Out loud?" Her eyebrows arched in a hopeful plea.

"Good try, Kassie. I think I'll take it to my room." I grabbed a box of tissues and headed down the hall. I had a feeling I'd need them.

I propped my pillows up and sat back on my bed. Ready or not, I was going to find out what he had to say. My fingers shook, and my heart galloped as I unfolded it.

Chrissy,

If you're already thinking of tearing this up, please don't. You never have to see me again, but please hear me out. It took me a long time to realize what I'd done to cause you to be so angry with me. Call me dense, but I think I've got it.

I raised my eyes to the ceiling. "Ha. Are you

kidding me? We stood right in front of your baby's mama's room and you took a long time to figure it out? Then after that you wanted to counsel me about my problems? Dense is an understatement." I nearly crumpled the letter, but curiosity urged me to see what *he* thought the problem was.

I guess I should have told you about the other woman in my life—the only other woman.

My stomach churned. That didn't sound good, but at least he was admitting it.

My younger sister, Breanna, has been through some rough times this past year.

Sister? Breanna was his sister? I slumped lower in my bed. I wanted to curl up and die. All the assumptions I'd made about him—and her—paraded through my mind. For some unknown reason I'd thought Decker was an only child.

During my final year of med school, she caught her husband cheating on her. It nearly did her in. She filed for divorce, but had to get a restraining order against him because he threatened to kill her if she left him. To top things off, she found out she was pregnant. My parents begged her to move to Chicago so they could take care of her. She should have, but she'd had an ugly fight with my dad a couple of years ago over Paul—the guy she married. Turns out Dad was right about him. That was a tough pill for Breanna to swallow. She also loved her job here and wanted to stay. The only option left was for me to take a break between med school and my residency and move here to watch out for her. Big brothers need to take care of their little sisters—even when they're stubborn. Her baby wasn't due until the twentieth.

On my birthday. Next week.

But I believe our trip to Chicago may have put her into early labor. Not the visit with our parents—that part was great, and Breanna patched things up with Dad. She plans to move there soon. Rather, the flight, so near her due date, put her into labor. That's why I was at the hospital when we last met. I've wondered ever since that time why you looked so sad. Even before we spoke, you had obviously been crying. My heart broke for you—especially since I realized I'd likely never find out. I want to be there for you, Chrissy. Not as a doctor (another thing I need to apologize for)—but as a friend.

My heart warmed and my skin tingled. I read on.

Years ago, Dr. Peterson attended med school with my father—yeah, he's a shrink, too. So when my dad apprised him of the Breanna situation, Dr. Peterson suggested I take some time off and do research in his office until Breanna was out of danger. That's where you came in.

I had to stop and get a drink of water. My mouth felt like cotton. I always misjudged people. Especially men.

If you're still reading, I am happily surprised. If you still hate me, then you'll want to stop now because I'm going to get real honest.

My heart beat a little faster. *Honesty is good.*

The main reason I went into psychiatry is because, before college, I went through some dark times of my own my when my twin brother drowned in a water-skiing accident. I have a hard time talking about this. I wish I could be more open, like you are. Please accept my apology for shutting down when you simply wanted to know about my life. I'm still healing.

I swallowed over the lump in my throat. Decker had lost someone, too.

Counseling really helped me. When I met you, I'd felt I met a kindred spirit. I'm sorry I never told you. I think I was afraid you'd think less of me. If we ever speak again, I'll share the details of my dark depression.

I shook my head. "No wonder you always made me do the talking."

I could tell you'd built some heavy-duty walls around your heart the first time we met. I made it my goal to break them down. Perhaps that was unfair if I didn't allow you the same courtesy. In the meantime, I was falling hard for you.

I dabbed at my burning eyes

Then came the kisses in the snow. Those kisses have both haunted and warmed me these past few weeks. I felt sure you were angry with me for kissing you—for moving too fast. Now, however, I'm hoping you were upset because you'd seen me with Breanna in the hospital and didn't know she's my sister. I'm an idiot not to have realized how that must have appeared sooner, but there it is.

Yup, you were an idiot. I blinked back new tears that had begun to form.

Still with me? I have to ask because after you rejected at least a hundred texts and calls, I'm doubtful you've read this far. If you have, thank you for hearing me out.

Chrissy, I feel responsible for your absence at the clinic. It seemed like you were doing so well—please reconsider and complete your treatment. If you don't want to see me, I'll find a different day to do my research. But don't do it for me, do it for yourself.

"I promise I will," I whispered.

If I never get a reply, I'll know you either didn't read the letter, truly believe that I'm an idiot and want nothing to do with me, or you just never cared the way I thought you did. Just know that I respect you and care for you very much.

Hopefully Yours,
Decker

Chapter Eleven

Perhaps my inner Elle kept me from grabbing my phone and dialing Decker's number. Or maybe my fear of commitment. No, I believed neither of them held me back. Some things seemed too good to be true. His letter fell into that category. I pinched myself to make sure I hadn't dreamt the whole thing. I didn't know how I could go from loathing the man for weeks to floating back up to that cloud 999 where I'd once blissfully resided. A complete U-turn was hard for me to make from one letter. I had to proceed with caution. I laughed at myself. Traffic signs were dictating my life.

My phone rang, jolting me from my ping-ponging thoughts. "Hi, Joy. What's up?"

"Chrissy, how's my favorite sister?"

I knew she needed a favor when she called me that. "Ha. Ha. What can I do for you?"

"Can you watch the boys tonight? I know it's last minute…" Her voice trailed off.

I had a feeling she had a date with Sean, the man she'd invited to Thanksgiving dinner, but I didn't want to say too much. She'd been really happy lately. A stark contrast to my dark state of mind—until today, that was. Babysitting my nephews always lifted my spirits.

"Sure, Joy, I can watch the boys. But can you do something for me?" I could almost hear her smile on the other end. All my sisters wanted to help me through my Decker-less days, as well as the holiday season in general.

"Anything. You name it."

"Can I come over early—like now—and talk?"

"Of course. Do you want to tell me what it's about, or keep me in suspense?

"Suspense." I laughed. "But don't worry, it's not bad. I just want you to read something and point me in the right direction."

She let out an audible sigh. I thought she was relieved I wasn't coming to cry on her shoulder. "I'd love to help."

I ended the call and sprinted through the apartment, gathering snacks and other Chrissy's-our-favorite-aunt paraphernalia.

Kassie watched me with a frown on her face. "Where are you going?"

"Oh, Joy called and needs a sitter."

"But the letter. Are you going to tell me what he said?"

I realized I'd been clutching the envelope in one hand while I'd gathered my things with the other, unwilling to let it out of my sight. I still wasn't sure Decker's words were real.

I looked at it and back at her. "I'll have to tell you later tonight."

"Just tell me if it's good news or bad." She smiled hopefully.

I gave her a thumbs up sign and ran out the door, headed for Joy's house and some sound advice.

"Chrissy." Joy pulled me through the door and gave me a quick hug. "Tell me what—"

I cut her off by handing her the letter. "Read it."

The boys were in the family room watching a movie, so we were able to huddle together on the couch while she read.

Of course Joy and the others had eventually dragged the Decker story out of me, and I knew they'd judged him harsher than anyone else. They had my back. I needed their brand of honesty right now, so I wouldn't make any mistakes. My heart was too tender for me to judge what to do on my own.

The letter was long, but geez Louise, the anticipation was killing me. "Are you praying about it, Joy?"

She chuckled and turned her eyes to me. "No, but what in the world is your question? This guy is amazing. All my doubts about his intentions have flown out the window."

A whoosh of air left my lungs. I guessed I'd been holding my breath awaiting her reaction. *So, he really is that good. Yes.*

"Should I ask Elle, too?"…Oops, wrong thing to have said to my oldest sister.

She frowned at me. "You don't trust me?"

"Of course I do. It's me I don't trust. I guess I'm scared about putting myself out there and getting hurt again. I don't think I can take it—especially during this time of year. Elle's had that kind of heartbreak."

Joy's eyes misted, which caused a lump to form in my throat. "Chrissy." Her voice just above a whisper. "You deserve to be happy. I've wondered if you knew that."

I squinted my eyes, giving her my best confused look. When she smiled that beautiful smile of hers, she reminded me of our mother. Sudden tears clouded my vision.

She pulled me into her arms, the way Mom would have. "You work so hard to bury your emotions. But sisters know. Especially sisters who have been through similar kinds of pain."

I held her back and stared at her. "Are you kidding? You've been through so much more than I have. How can you even compare? Part of my struggle comes from watching how well you, Elle, and Holly have handled things compared to me. I just can't get rid of the pain." *Or the guilt.*

"That. That right there is your problem, Chrissy. You think everyone else has the right to hurt worse than you, but you're wrong. We all hurt, but in different ways. I have Charlie and the twins. You have no idea what a comfort they are to me. Elle has Tatum."

"But—" I couldn't hold the truth in another minute. Joy would hate me—all my sisters would, but I had to say it. "I killed them, Joy. I killed them."

Her brows pulled down in anger, her eyes narrowed, piercing me to the core. She hated me and I deserved it. "What are you talking about, Chrissy? You think you killed Mom and Dad? No. Their accident was caused by icy roads and bad drivers. You had nothing to do with it." Her gentle tone sounded nothing like I'd expected. That was because she still didn't know the truth.

"Joy, do you remember the events of that day?"

"I don't think I'll ever forget a single second of that day."

"Then you remember that I had come home for Christmas break from school really sick."

"Yes, you had strep throat. Could hardly get out of

bed. I felt horrible for you. I also remember you feeling a bit better that day and had planned to come to our family dinner at mine and Tom's house."

"Except that dinner never happened because of me."

Joy's forehead wrinkled. "Huh?"

"Because I had to have a strawberry shake. My throat hurt so badly, and only a shake sounded good to me." I burst into tears. I'd promised myself to never tell anyone the truth because it was so ugly. I'd also vowed to never forgive myself. My selfishness had caused my parents' deaths. "Don't you see? Mom and Dad drove clear across town to my favorite fast-food restaurant to buy me a stupid milkshake. I'm the reason they died. I was so selfish."

Joy shook her head. "Are you serious right now? Is that why you have punished yourself all these years? Because we all knew about the strawberry shake, Chrissy."

My body jolted. "You what?"

"Uh-huh. And while they were out, Mom promised to pick up a pound of butter for me, and Dad was going to stop at the auto shop to check on Holly's car. And before they got to her place, Elle had Tatum ready to go with them on their errands. The detour to get your shake probably saved Tatum's life. Mom and Dad were always there for *all* of us. That's why we miss them so badly."

I struggled to wrap my mind around Joy's words. All this time I'd imagined I had sent my parents to their deaths. "So I'm not completely responsible for the accident?" My words came out between sobbing hiccups.

"Not even remotely. Think about where the accident occurred—they were miles from that fast-food restaurant."

I'd honestly never considered their location in relation to the restaurant—had just made an assumption, as usual.

Joy scooped me into a tight hug. "You've got to let this go, Chrissy. You deserve happiness. We all do."

A burden of enormous proportions lifted off my shoulders. "Thank you, Joy."

She loosened her grip on me and waved the letter in the air. So…about this Decker."

I laughed and wiped away my tears. "Yeah…the reason I'm here."

"If he is half as good as he sounds, you need to let him know how you feel… You do have feelings for him, don't you?"

I hesitated.

Joy tilted her head and narrowed her eyes. "Be honest with yourself. You have to pretend that you never saw him with that girl…uh…"

"Breanna," I supplied.

"Yes. It's not fair to him if you continue to let those negative and false feelings cloud your judgment. Look at what he's done for her. Don't you want a man who would do as much, or more, for you?"

A fresh tear made a path down my cheek. Joy was right. I had been so unfair to Decker. He'd not meant for me to see him with Breanna and make all kinds of assumptions about him. I nodded, not trusting myself to speak. Of course I wanted all that in a guy, but I didn't know if I deserved it. Especially after I'd pushed him away so forcefully.

Joy must have been able to read my mind. "Things aren't broken beyond repair." She waved the letter again. "He obviously still wants you."

"So should I call him?"

She looked up to the heavens and shook her head, then pulled my phone from my bag. "Yes. Right now, while I get ready for my evening out."

"You have a date—lucky Sean."

Joy turned red. "Call him." She shoved the phone into my hands.

Even though I'd deleted his number, I knew it by heart. My fingers shook as I punched it in.

After one ring, I nearly hit the "end call" button, but he answered. Oh my gosh. Caramel smoothness melted through my phone.

"Chrissy, are you there?"

I realized I hadn't responded to his "Hello." "Yeah, I'm here. Sorry. Um…I got your letter." I began to pace to relieve the nervous anxiety thrumming in my heart.

Decker didn't say anything, clearly waiting for me to go on.

"Can we talk?" I held my breath.

"I'd like that. How soon? I'm available this evening."

I let the breath go. I almost said to come get me right then, but I remembered why I was at Joy's house. "I'm babysitting tonight. My sister has a date."

"Need help?"

"Really? I'd love some help. But I have to warn you—it gets crazy around here. In fact, my sister calls the twins her little hoodlums. If that doesn't scare you away, you're a strong man." I laughed.

He didn't.

"Waiting this long to hear your voice hasn't scared me away, Chrissy. I think I can handle it." His voice sounded friendly, but serious.

I had hurt him. I might have set myself up for an ambush. At least I'd have the boys as a buffer if things went south. Fear twisted my heart. "You know, we don't have to meet tonight. We can talk another ti—"

"Oh no you don't. You're not getting out of it that easily. Text me your sister's address, and I'll head over."

"Okay. Bye, Decker."

Joy must have been listening in the next room. She rushed in and grabbed my shoulders. "What did he say?"

"Is it okay with you if he helps me babysit tonight?"

You'd think Joy had won the lottery by the loud whoop she let out. Her broad smile warmed my heart. "Absolutely." She looked at the clock, then hurried down the hall toward her room. "Gotta get ready now," she yelled before disappearing through the door.

She came out in a red dress I'd never seen before. Joy didn't buy new clothes for herself often. This guy must be special. She even had a bright red manicure to match. *Hmm.*

"By the way, Joy, you look amazing. He's a lucky guy." I winked.

She gave me a shove. "Well, thank you, but I believe I'm the lucky one."

Before we could get into details of her love life, a sportscar drove up and she hurried out the door. *I hope he treats her well*, I thought. *She deserves to be happy, too.*

Only moments later I found myself embroiled in a serious game with the boys.

"You have to find me first." Charlie whizzed past me as I counted to twenty with my eyes closed.

"Nineteen and twenty. Ready or not, here I come." I opened my eyes and looked around. Four little feet poked out from beneath the curtain that covered the sliding glass door. Only toes—adorable toes. I smothered a laugh and crept quietly to the door. "Hmm, I wonder where Micah and Mitchell are." I heard them trying to contain their giggles, and I smiled as I imagined their tense little faces. Finally, I pulled the drape open and yelled, "Gotcha." They squealed in delight and grabbed my legs.

"How'd you find us, Aunt Kissy?" Micah asked. They tackled me to the ground, and I let them. Who didn't like being attacked by three-year-olds? They loved you even when you messed up. I pulled them both into a bear hug. I didn't know why, but I wanted to cry. Something about those innocent little guys melted my heart.

Mitchell looked around. "What about Charlie?"

"I guess we'd better find him." We got up and they each put a chubby hand in mine. We were off and running.

We didn't get too far before the doorbell rang. I froze. I hadn't forgotten about Decker. He'd been constantly on my mind ever since our phone conversation. I'd just sorely underestimated how long it would take him to get to Joy's house. I hadn't even had a chance to look in a mirror to see what condition I was in after all the crying I'd done, then the twin-attack.

Charlie materialized from his hiding place and

opened the door before I could think of my next move, which would have been to sprint to the bathroom and brush my hair.

Chapter Twelve

Decker stood in the doorway.

I was rooted in place with four little eyes staring up at me.

"Aunt Chrissy, I think it's for you," Charlie said, opening the door wide to let the man in.

Beneath his leather bomber jacket he wore an aqua-colored shirt that made his dark eyes irresistibly beautiful.

"You must be Charlie." Decker held out his hand. Charlie shook it.

"Very nice to meet you, Mr. Decker."

I stifled a laugh. Charlie was such a little man. I knew Joy had been working with him on his manners. I made a mental note to tell her how well he'd done.

The twins immediately left my side and ran to shake Decker's hand, too—traitors!

Once they'd all finished trying to impress the new guy, the boys allowed Decker to get past the threshold.

"Hi, Chrissy."

I self-consciously ran my fingers through my hair in an attempt to coax it back in place.

Decker chuckled, so I quit.

"We've been—"

Mitchell cut me off. "We've been attacking Aunt Kissy."

As if that were the signal, Mitchell and Micah

yelled in unison, "Twin attack." They both pounced on me all over again.

Oh man, this was going to be a long night.

Decker didn't run away. That was the good news. In fact, he chuckled and began tickling the boys.

In fits of laughter, the twins finally cried uncle and sprinted for safety.

"Thank you," I said from my toppled-over position on the floor.

Decker held out a hand to help me up from the ground.

"I told you they're wild."

Seven-year-old Charlie, ever the man of the house since his father died, turned sober eyes on me and said, "Don't worry, Aunt Chrissy. I'll take them with me to watch a movie. That will calm them down before bedtime."

I pulled him closer and whispered in his ear, "You know you're my favorite, right?"

He giggled and whispered back, "You know that *I* know you say that to all of us, right?"

I swatted him playfully as he scooted off to round up the hoodlum twins. "Have them brush their teeth and put on their jammies before you start the movie," I hollered.

I waited in the hallway until I heard the toilet flush and the faucet shut off—not that I didn't trust Charlie.

Decker was the man I was uncertain of.

We were alone now—well, relatively. And with *Alien Dinosaurs* playing in the background, the mood was set.

"Can I get you a soda or anything?" I asked Decker.

He shook his head. "I'm fine. Do you think we're safe to talk?"

"Yeah. The twins always fall asleep watching movies. We're good for a while."

We sat on the loveseat. My heart thudded. Decker sat close and smelled so good—spicy-fresh again—I wanted to cry. Well, maybe not cry, but he did smell that good. He smiled and moved an errant strand of hair from my face. His hand lingered on the side of my cheek, sending a million sparks from my head to my toes.

"I'm sorry I messed everything up. I thought you were married—or had a girlfriend." The words spilled from my nervous lips.

"I'm the idiot," he said. "I should have put it together sooner. But I have to ask why you would assume I was married because I was at the hospital? Besides the fact that I was helping with the birth of a baby, of course."

His expression was hard to read, but I thought he realized that helping with a woman's birthing experience was not typical, unless you were the father—or her OB.

He raised his eyebrows, as in "oh, I get it."

"Well, there also was The Olive Garden."

His forehead wrinkled. "Huh? The Olive Garden?"

I finally spilled it all, from the conversation I'd overheard between the receptionists to the lunch at The Olive Garden to the hospital where he'd helped his sister—yeah, it took a while to get it all out, but I did. "And now you know I'm crazy—or at least very insecure." I looked down, embarrassed. "But you probably knew that from the beginning, I guess."

I wished I could see his face. But I was too busy hanging my head in shame. I wondered if he was glancing at the door, calculating his getaway, or more likely, staring at me, thinking I was a dork.

I didn't have to wonder long, as warm arms pulled me to him. "Chrissy." He chuckled. "That's what I love about you."

I looked up at his face, so close to mine, which was a mistake because it put me in a trance of sorts. "Huh? You love that I'm a jealous, insecure—"

He cut me off in the best way possible. With his lips. He kissed me softly, then said in a low voice, "You talk too much." Then he kissed me again, wrapping his arms tighter around me.

I kissed him back, enjoying every second of the fireworks exploding in my heart.

When we broke apart, he said, "What I meant by that is, I love how once you recognized what you did wrong, or in this case, misunderstood, you weren't too prideful to admit it. I wish I were more like that."

He had just turned my shortcomings into compliments. "Now you talk too much." I snaked my arms around his neck and pulled him in for more kisses.

He laughed against my lips and the vibration shook the house—or at least my heart.

"Aunt Chrissy?" Uh oh, that wasn't Decker.

I quickly untangled my arms from Decker's neck and turned in the direction of the little voice.

"What is it, Charlie?" I tried to act natural, although I knew my face must be hot pink.

"Micah and Mitch are asleep on the bean bag chairs. Can I turn off the movie and go to bed?"

"Of course you can. Want to be tucked in?"

Charlie frowned at me. "I'm not a baby. I can brush my teeth and say my prayers and tuck myself in." He let out a huff, then smiled, showing those cute dimples I loved.

I smothered a laugh at my very big little nephew. "Okay, then. I at least need a hug goodnight." I pulled him in close and kissed him on the head. "Sleep well, little man."

"Good night, Aunt Chrissy. Good night, Uncle Decker."

Uncle Decker? Oh no. I clapped a hand over my mouth and heat rose to my cheeks.

Decker, on the other hand, acted completely nonchalant. "Good night, Charlie. I hope to see you again very soon."

Charlie disappeared.

I looked at Decker. "I'm sorry about that. He's smart, but sometimes he gets things mixed up."

"Maybe he knows something we don't." He winked at me.

Fireworks exploded again as my heart soared into outer space.

Decker helped me move the twins into their bunks. He looked so natural with a toddler cuddled in his arms.

Returning to the couch, Decker took my hand. "Maybe we should stick to talking." He chuckled. "Though I prefer what we were doing before."

I agreed. We still needed to discuss so many things, not to mention the fact that Joy could walk in at any moment.

Turned out, we had a couple of hours before that sister of mine found her way back home. And Decker and I…mostly talked…mostly.

****

Monday morning was frosty, everywhere except in my heart. I had Decker to thank for that. On my way to work, I picked up Melba Teague. Screening day had arrived for the Doggone It commercial. She needed to give us the thumbs up—or down. Somehow, despite Ashlyn's absence, we'd managed to pull the campaign together before the deadline. That was, if Melba approved. I was nervous, but ready to see the presentation come together.

Mr. Hobbs, Mr. Bevins, Melba, Cole, and I convened in the conference room. A screen magically descended from the ceiling. Before showing the commercial, I explained our strategy to send out mailers, as well as put coupons in Valu-packs. I passed around examples of both. Then the time had come for what we'd all worked so hard on.

Cole dimmed the lights and the commercial began. I crossed my fingers and sent a prayer heavenward.

At the end, with the Doggone It jingle still playing, everyone started to clap. I turned to Melba. She was the one whose opinion I truly cared about. Tears glistened in her eyes. Not what I'd expected. She either loved it or hated it.

"Melba, are you all right?"

She squeezed my hand and nodded her head. I handed her a tissue.

"It's so wonderful what y'all have done fer me. Did you see how pretty I looked?"

Now *I* needed a tissue. "Melba, you *are* pretty. Inside and out. I'm so happy you liked it. And while the others are off congratulating themselves, let me take this opportunity to thank you for allowing me to work with you—and even more, for being my friend. You mean a lot to me, and I hope we can stay close forever."

Oops—maybe I should have saved that for a more private moment.

Melba let out a few loud sobs and clutched me to her. I wrapped my arms around her in return. I didn't know who'd benefitted most from our work together, Melba or me.

Mr. Hobbs interrupted our moment. "Mrs. Teague, with your approval we'll move forward with this campaign."

Melba nodded yes, beaming through her tears.

"It will be a week before it airs, but I'll start the wheels in motion today," he added.

"Mr. Hobbs," I said, "I have a few things I need to discuss with Mrs. Teague. You go ahead and get those wheels spinning. I'll be out of the office for a while." I didn't usually talk to my boss so boldly, but I'd pulled off a minor miracle and needed to celebrate with the star of the show.

"Well…er…okay. I guess we can proceed without you."

I turned to Melba. "Ready, my friend?"

She took me by the arm as if she knew what I'd planned. I didn't even know what I'd planned, but we had to do something to celebrate; plus, I wanted to fill her in on how things had worked out with Decker—scratch that—*were* working out with Decker. Still too early to know if things had actually worked out, but I liked the direction they'd taken.

She slid into my car. "Olive Garden?" I said.

She chuckled. "Olive Garden."

****

I climbed into bed that night thinking of how wonderfully things had gone with Melba. Her business was running smoothly now with the help of an office manager, and more clients would be coming her way. She looked fantastic, thanks to Ashlyn, and she had friends who truly cared about her.

I had to keep the positive thoughts coming because the next day, December twentieth, was my birthday. Sigh. Most people would be excited about that, but I wanted to hide somewhere. Having my birthday in December, so close to the anniversary of my parents' fatal accident, made it anything but happy. My mom used to make such a big deal over birthdays. I knew I was old enough to get over not having her homemade birthday cake, but it hurt to not have her there for me anymore.

Now that the Doggone It campaign was winding down, I couldn't bury myself in work. Maybe I should take the day off and stay in bed. The idea seemed appealing.

The next morning, I woke up at six o'clock, as always. I planned my speech to Mr. Hobbs as to why I couldn't come in, then tried snoozing for another hour. No luck. Well, if I was up anyway, I may as well go to work, I decided.

I took extra care getting ready. After all, today was my birthday and that made me a whole year older than I had been just a few hours before. I should probably treat myself to some wrinkle cream or something. I laughed. I wore an ivory-colored sweater dress that cinched in at the waist, accentuating my figure. Beneath my dress, I pulled on some ribbed leggings, then added my favorite brown leather boots. I curled my long hair into loose spirals, something I only did for special occasions because it took so much time. Then I made sure my makeup enhanced my every feature. I appraised myself in the mirror. "You look pretty good for the ripe old age of twenty-four," I said to my reflection. I pulled on my dress-length, green wool jacket and tied a colorful scarf around my neck. Happy birthday to me, I thought as I left my apartment.

As I turned the key to lock the door, I sensed someone behind me.

"Hello, birthday girl."

Chapter Thirteen

"Decker! What are you doing here?" I allowed him to pull me in for an embrace.

He looked at my lips, which were slick with gloss, then kissed me anyway. Best birthday present ever.

"I thought you might be holing up, so I came to keep you company."

I shrugged and displayed my I-don't-know-what-you're-talking-about face.

He chuckled. "Have you forgotten that you've told me how difficult birthdays have been—at least the last few?"

I wanted to tell him how good it felt to have someone in my life—in addition to my sisters—who knew that about me, and why. Instead I pulled the lapels of his coat until his face met mine again. This time I gave him a passionate kiss he'd not soon forget.

"Wow. I think I'll surprise you more often."

Heat rushed to my face, which was already warm from that fiery kiss.

"Where are you headed? You look fantastic."

"I tried playing hooky from work, but my heart wasn't in it this year. I think you've cured me." I gave him a saucy smile.

"Well, it so happens that no one's expecting you at work today."

"How do you know that?"

"Because the receptionist told me you left a message early this morning and wouldn't be in." He looked at me like I'd lost my jellybeans.

"I did?" I pulled out my phone and saw that I actually had called in. I thought I'd dreamed it. "Hmm, I really am getting old."

He laughed. "Now that you're all ready for the day, what'll it be? It just so happens I have the day off, too."

I thought for a few minutes. "This will sound strange, Decker, but do you think we could go see your sister, Breanna?"

His eyes widened as his face split into a huge grin.

I went on. "It's just that I've misjudged so many people lately—including her. And I don't even know her. Honestly, I've found getting to know people—I mean, *really* know people, like Melba Teague—has been more therapeutic than all those years of counseling."

He looked at me with intense, sparkling brown eyes. I wished I could read his mind. He raised his hand to my cheek and ran a thumb along my jaw. "One more reason for me to love you, Chrissy," he said in a low, extra-smooth voice. He tilted my face to meet his and kissed me again.

This time I let the tingling sensation vibrate clear to my toes.

When we'd both recovered, he added, "She'll be excited to meet you and show off that little guy of hers."

"Oh, and let's stop at a store. I know of a little boutique on Academy that has the cutest baby things. I want to get her a gift."

Decker smiled, took me by the hand, and led me to

his car.

****

Breanna was adorable. Well, I already knew that, but she had a personality to match her pretty face. And that baby…so cute. He had the roundest blue eyes, and I swore he smiled when I held him. I was a little disappointed that she planned to move back to Chicago soon, just as I was finally getting to know her. I was so glad we spent a couple of hours visiting.

Decker treated me to lunch at the Broadmoor. I suggested the Mason Jar, but he said he wanted to take me somewhere I didn't go often. The Broadmoor was definitely classy—and pricey.

Over his steak and my salad, I asked him to tell me about Dallas, his twin brother. I hoped he'd open up to me this time.

He hesitated, then cleared his throat. "Dallas loved water-skiing—we both did." The story went on. They had been skiing when something in the water snagged Dallas' ski, flipping him into the air before pulling him under. Decker had been in the boat with his dad, waiting for Dallas to surface. "We'd circled around to get him, but when he came up, he was lifeless." Decker's voice cracked as tears glistened in his eyes.

Moisture slid down my own cheeks, as well.

His hands grasped mine across the table. "He'd apparently hit his head on something pretty hard— likely his ski. We never found out for sure. Blunt force trauma was all the autopsy report revealed."

"You witnessed his death, then." I couldn't keep a sob from escaping. His memories combined with my own were overwhelming. His story didn't end there. My heart overflowed with emotion when he trusted me with the rest—the darkness that had nearly taken him down.

"After the accident, I felt like I'd drowned with my brother—I'd actually wished that I had. It was so painful. We'd done everything together. I'd wake up nights gasping for air." Decker's grip on my hands tightened. "My dad had been pretty torn up about losing Dallas, too, but thanks to his training in psychiatry, he'd known the signs—my signs—of depression. You know the kind I'm talking about."

I nodded. I knew exactly the kind he was talking about—suffocating darkness that stripped you of your will to live.

"Dad set me up with some heavy-duty counseling. It probably saved my life." Decker's gaze dropped to our hands, still clasped firmly together. He swallowed and looked back up at me, then inclined his head and lowered his voice. "Dallas talks to me. Just a whisper now and then. You know, words of encouragement. I...feel him with me." His eyes narrowed. "Do you think I'm crazy for believing that?"

Of course not, I thought, but the words were stuck in my throat. I shook my head. When the words finally made their way out, they sounded foreign to me. "My mother speaks to me, too." My skin prickled. She was with me. I always imagined she had been, but now I knew it.

Decker brought both of my hands to his mouth and kissed my fingers. "I love you, Chrissy."

"I love you, too." Fresh tears splashed down my cheeks.

I could tell it had been difficult for Decker to share the story of Dallas' tragic death, and even harder admitting to the depression which had followed, but I also knew how therapeutic talking about it could be. We cried together. I had never been so connected to a man.

As we waited for our bill, I caught a whiff of a familiar cologne. Not Decker's spicy-fresh scent, but I recognized it. Then a hearty laugh rang out—a laugh I knew well. I started to stand, but just as quickly, sat back down and listened.

"I'll be in Berlin by Tuesday. Your half of the money will be in your off-shore account by noon tomorrow," a male voice said.

"Pleasure doing business with you," replied another.

Decker's forehead creased. "What's wrong?"

I let out several nervous breaths, then held a finger to my lips. I dipped my head to the side and there I saw it on the ground, behind my seat. A leather briefcase nestled mere feet from my chair. The embossed name "Lyonstone, LLC" jumped out and nearly knocked me over, confirming what I'd seen. I turned back to face Decker and covered my mouth to smother a gasp.

Decker narrowed his eyes in confusion.

"Do you think you could meet me outside? I'm going to slip out the side exit. I'll explain later."

He tilted his head and furrowed his brow but nodded.

I quietly exited the restaurant and began pacing the pavement, waiting for Decker. My heart hurt. We'd been so betrayed. I knew my sisters had, had doubts about Uncle Simon's motives, but I so deeply wanted him to fill the hole in my heart. Why would he do such a thing? I supposed he'd burned through his inheritance, and greed dictated his actions.

What really hurt, however, was the man he dined with. Our attorney, Richard Arnett. And now I knew how Simon got to the money…with our lawyer's help.

Decker finally made it out and pulled me into his arms. "What happened?"

I was too angry to fall apart. I ranted instead.

"My Uncle Simon and our family lawyer Mr. Arnett are in cahoots." I pushed out of his arms and kicked a rock, sending it skittering across the parking lot. My pacing resumed.

"Slow down, Chrissy." Decker stood in my path and turned me to look him in the eyes. "They are the reason the foundation funds were frozen?"

"Yes. I heard my uncle laugh and caught a few phrases. I stood to talk to him, but before he saw me, I realized who he was with. That briefcase by my chair…the one with Lyonstone embossed on the front…belongs, I assume, to the man who set everything up—the man who robbed us—my long-lost uncle. And he was dining with Mr. Arnett."

Decker pulled me close.

Too angry to be consoled yet, I initially resisted, then gave in.

"Breathe, Chrissy." He rubbed my back until I regained some control.

I explained everything to him as we drove to my apartment first, to get my copies of the lawyer-supplied—or rather, traitor-supplied—Frost Foundation documents. Oh, how he had us all fooled. I forced back tears. Then on to the police department. Sharing my burden with Decker helped. He gave me suggestions, and he advised me to keep my heart out of it as much as possible. Easier said than done.

Officer Nelson showed us to his desk, where I gave him the scoop. "I doubt they're still dining at the Broadmoor, but I have contact information for both of them," I said. My uncle's laugh still rang in my ears.

"I'm on it." Officer Nelson took the numbers and the envelope of detailed documents my sisters and I each had copies of, then showed us out.

Decker closed the door behind the detective. "What are you smiling about?"

I shrugged. "I guess I never thought I'd be the one to solve the mystery. Maybe now construction on the hospital wing can resume."

He bent his head and kissed me. "Are you going to call your sisters?"

"Umm, not yet." I kissed him again. "Let's get out of here."

I was determined to push the matter aside for the remainder of my birthday.

It worked. Our time spent together was magical. But I still worried—hoping nothing else would spoil it. We sat on the sofa in my apartment. The television hummed softly in the background while we talked.

"So I've applied for my residency."

Boom! It happened. My happiness was about to tell me he was moving away. I tried not to let the disappointment show in my face. After all, I knew he'd always planned to finish his schooling, and his residency was the last step to becoming Dr. Decker—

"Decker, do you know, after all this time, I don't know your last name?" Seriously. I was falling in love with a guy who'd never mentioned his last name. I turned to face him.

He laughed.

"Why are you laughing?"

He stopped, at least with his mouth. His eyes still danced with amusement. "Chrissy, I've never told you my last name because you're going to hate it."

"That's ridiculous. Why would I hate your name? I guess I would hate calling you Doctor Doolittle—it's not that, is it?"

He shook his head, laughing again.

"Doctor Frankenstein? Doctor Kevorkian? What is it? I'm not going to guess every horrible name there is. Besides, if it belongs to you, I'll love it."

"Trust me, you've already told me how much you hate it."

My forehead creased, and I squinted my eyes in concentration. I had never told him I hated his last name.

He leaned over and kissed me. "It's okay. You're going to have to hear it at some point. "My full name is Decker William...Snow."

My jaw went slack. "No way."

He chuckled. "Told you."

"It's a good thing you've cured me of my snow-phobia." I pictured that wonderful snowball fight, and the magical kisses that had followed.

"In more ways than one, I hope." He scooped me into a hug.

When he loosened his grip, I had to ask, "So..." The question stuck in my throat.

"So...what? Were you going to say something?

"Yes...where did you apply for your residency?"

The laughter in his eyes died. "Everywhere. I should have sent the papers in months ago, but I wasn't sure about leaving Breanna. Now that she and my dad have patched things up, I went ahead and applied."

But now you're leaving me, I thought, but I couldn't say it. He'd sacrificed so much for his family. I didn't need to add guilt to his burden. I could feel my eyes getting watery.

"My father has some pull in the world of psychiatry and is trying to get the process expedited. I'm hoping to hear something by Christmas."

"So soon." That was all I could muster. I wanted to say I was happy for him, but I wasn't. I turned away so he couldn't see the tears that were about to lose their fight with gravity.

"Ahh! That was dumb of me." He gently pulled my face back where he could look me in the eyes. "I could have waited to tell you on a day other than your birthday. I'm such an idiot sometimes." He wiped the moisture from my cheeks with his thumb. "I'm so sorry, Chrissy."

"It's okay." It wasn't okay. It was anything but okay. If Decker left, I would survive. I knew I would— I'd grown so much and come so far in the last few months. But I'd also found a happiness I'd never known existed—a love deeper than I'd ever experienced before. I would survive, but it would hurt to give that feeling up—to give him up.

Chapter Fourteen

For my own closure, I needed to confront the men I'd come to view as father figures. Luckily, they were being held in a lockup nearby. I was allowed to sit across a table from both and let my anger and hurt loose on them.

"We trusted you, Mr. Arnett—with everything."

He wouldn't make eye contact with me and didn't say a word. Just stared at the table.

"And you, Uncle Simon. You deceived me in the worst way—"

He cut me off. "You and your sisters have great jobs. I am entitled to that money." His eyes slanted and his lips pulled down into a sneer. Gone was the man I'd thought resembled my father. This man was a stranger.

"You were given half of the inheritance. Where is it?" I skewered him with a glare.

"I don't have to answer to you." He stood and turned toward the warden. "We're done here."

The guard ushered me out, but I looked back at the men one last time. "Dad trusted you, Mr. Arnett." I shook my head. "But Dad never said a word about you, Simon. Now I know why."

****

"I'll get back to you by the end of the day, Ms. Frost." Nathan Klein, Attorney at Law, shook my hand.

I let out a breath of relief. "Thank you so much.

This means the world to me and my sisters."

My surprisingly smooth appointment was over less than an hour after it'd begun. Things were going to be easier to resolve than expected. I'd been tempted to call my sisters and report the news, but after meeting with Mr. Klein, I thought it would be a great Christmas surprise. After all, they'd each spent many hours, blood, sweat, and tears helping me through the last four years. Time to give back.

Hopefully, I could keep the good news under wraps for a few more days.

Decker and I decided to spend as much time together as possible, for now, and I was determined to not let my crazy head get in the way of enjoying it. We both hated the fact that he'd be going off to Timbuctoo soon, but things were only made worse when we tried to talk about it. Thank goodness the Doggone It campaign was finished. Now I had time to take long lunch hours so we could eat together, and I could leave work early to spend my evenings with him.

Besides the fact that the one man I'd fallen in love with was about to disappear and the Frost girls had been betrayed by our uncle and trusted attorney, life was good. I hadn't had any panic attacks since the hospital incident, and I was pretty sure I no longer hated snow. But the best thing about this year—besides Decker, of course—had to be Melba Teague, my new friend and mother figure...sort of. Nobody could take the place of my real mom, but Melba's big heart brought her pretty darn close. If I've learned one thing, it was how much we missed out on when we judged others. If I'd learned two things, it was how much we could forget our own problems when we concentrated on someone else's. If

I'd learned three things, it was how corny I sounded when I waxed philosophically. And if I'd learned four things—

"Chrissy?" Decker stood at my front door. It was a good thing, too, because I didn't really have a fourth thing.

"Oh good, you're here."

He hugged me, then held me back and studied my eyes. "How do you want to spend Christmas Eve day?"

I knew why he'd asked me so earnestly. After all, my track record for the past few years suggested today would be a dark one, but if anyone had figured out how to get me through it, Decker had. "Let's spend it by not checking the mail, for starters."

He chuckled, but I was serious.

I'd reached the day before Christmas and hadn't broken down yet. That was some sort of miracle. If he found out about his residency today, I didn't think I could take it.

I forced myself to stay in present time. "We could finish shopping. I know it's Christmas Eve, so the stores are bound to be crazy, but I still need some things for Holly and Elle."

"Shopping it is."

"Has your family forgiven you for staying here instead of going home?" It had been his idea to stay in Colorado for Christmas, but I felt a twinge of guilt.

"I'm not worried. They finally have Breanna home, plus their first grandchild. I doubt they'll even notice I'm missing."

I will, I thought as my stomach took a flip.

We headed to the Citadel for some last-minute items. Walking hand in hand with Decker through the

Christmas-bedazzled mall was amazing. I'd gotten so used to ordering everything online, I'd forgotten how magical the holiday season truly could be—even the commercialized part of it. I wanted to stop at every display and soak it all in.

Decker's grin never left his face.

I knew what he was thinking—that I was like a little kid. And he was right. Welcoming Christmas back into my life, after a four-year hiatus, was a gift all its own. We shopped until my arms were loaded down with way more gifts than I'd ever intended to buy.

"If I'd known how easy it is to entertain you at a mall, I would have brought you here sooner," he teased. "Do you want to sit on Santa's lap, too?"

I punched him on the shoulder. "I would, but I think it's too late for Santa to get me what I want for Christmas."

"And what is that?" His voice turned gentle.

"You know what it is, Decker. And I know I'm selfish for even wishing for it." I swallowed hard and blinked back tears. No way would I let my fear of him leaving ruin this perfect day.

"It's never too late to wish." He bent his head down and kissed me.

"Whatever," I whispered.

"You look tired. Do you want to sit on one of those seats?" He motioned to a set of comfortable-looking, over-stuffed chairs by a Christmas tree.

The lights winked at me, nearly putting the smile back on my face.

"Okay, but I think the mall is about to close. It's Christmas Eve, after all." I glanced around. "I think we're the last two shoppers here." Everyone had left to get home to their families.

We both took a seat in the comfy chairs.

"That reminds me." He hopped back on his feet. "I ordered some gifts for my family from a store around the corner. I'm pretty sure they were shipped, but I'd like to double check. Do you mind? I'll only be a minute."

I shook my head, then let it fall against the soft chair back while he ran his errand. I closed my eyes and pretended the day would never end and Decker would never leave.

I must have dozed off for a few minutes. Something nudged my leg, startling me out of my sweet dreams. "What?" I jerked my leg away. Then I noticed what had bumped me, which made me even more perplexed. The cutest Golden Retriever puppy stared up at me with big brown eyes. "Oh, hi, sweet little guy, did you escape from the pet store?" I picked him up and cuddled him. "You are so cute."

He licked my nose and his collar scratched me. Wait. Not his collar, but something attached to it.

I held him up to take a look. Dangling from the buckle was a ring. I pulled him in for an even closer inspection. *What in the world?*

Before I could catch my breath, I heard, "Merry Christmas, Chrissy." Decker dropped to one knee. "Will you marry me?"

I must have looked surprised, confused, and thrilled all at once, because that was how I felt. "But how?"

"Not exactly what I'd hoped you'd say."

I laughed nervously, and heat rose to my face. "I mean, yes. Absolutely yes. But still, how?"

The puppy squirmed in my arms, and Decker set him down and wrapped his leash around the chair leg. He tugged an envelope from his jacket pocket. "This came yesterday. I thought it would go well with my Christmas gift to you."

My hands shook as I opened the letter. The words "Residency" and "Denver, Colorado" popped out at me. "You're going to do your residency in Denver?"

He smiled that Decker-liscious smile that had first claimed my heart, then scooted next to me and gave me a long, sweet kiss. "I love you, Chrissy."

The mall whirled around me like a merry-go-round. Colors, lights, music, and now a diamond ring. But best of all, I had Decker. "I love you, too."

"What do you want to name him?"

I'd almost forgotten about the puppy. "That's easy."

Decker's eyebrows arched. "Oh?"

"Yeah. His name is Caramel."

****

On Christmas morning, when Joy opened the door to welcome me, her mouth gaped open as she saw Decker and Melba standing beside me—Caramel in my arms.

"Merry Christmas, Joy." I couldn't help but beam at the happiness shining on her face. "I hope it's okay that I brought some friends."

"Merry Christmas yourself, Chrissy." She ushered us in. "Mrs. Teague, Decker, this is a pleasant surprise. And I assume the puppy was a gift?"

I nodded. "Do you think he can stay here for a few months? I kept him in my apartment last night because Kassie's out of town. Besides the fact that pets are not allowed, she's deathly allergic to them. But he's so cute." I nuzzled him close to my cheek.

Joy laughed. "He's adorable, and the boys will be thrilled to have a puppy around the house, if they don't torture him with love."

Melba spoke up. "How about ya let me take care of 'im? It'll be my gift to you. After all, Doggone It is one of the best boarding places in town; haven't ya seen the ads?" She winked and we all laughed.

I wanted to kiss her. I actually did trust her more with my new little treasure than those three crazy nephews of mine. Plus, I really didn't want to burden Joy.

"But what do you think will change in a few months?" Joy tickled Caramel under his chin.

"Oh." I giggled nervously. "This." I held up my left hand, where a sparkling diamond donned my ring finger. "I see a pet-friendly apartment in my near future."

Joy looked from me to Decker, and a huge grin spread across her face. She gathered us both—all three, if you count Caramel—into a hug. She whispered in my ear, "I'm so happy for you, Chrissy." When she finally let go, there were happy tears brimming her eyes. She hugged Melba, too, and thanked her for offering to save her from puppy-training. "Go on into the family room. I'll be right behind you."

Melba hung back to ask Joy what she could do to help with our annual Christmas breakfast. "Let me at least do the dishin' up," she insisted.

While we walked down the hallway, I noticed Decker looking up at the arched entry to the family room. A mistletoe twirled merrily as warm air from the heat register made it dance. The gleam in his eye was unmistakable. Nor was it deniable.

"Don't you dare take another step." His voice was still irresistibly velvety-smooth.

"But what if someone—"

Decker tugged the puppy from my arms and set him down before I could finish my sentence. Then he put both hands on my cheeks and bent his head to meet mine.

As his warm lips found their target, I didn't care who caught us. Today was Christmas, after all.

Voices sounded from the other side of the archway. "Woohoo, Chrissy and Decker."

I ducked my head, knowing full-well how red my face was. "I told you so," I mumbled. He didn't seem to let anything embarrass him. Wait 'til we went to see his family. I could get him back then.

He laced his fingers with mine and led me into the room.

Looking around, I realized the mistletoe had probably been well-used by the time we'd arrived. Many happy smiles greeted us. Sean, who had made Joy so happy and whom we'd all come to love. And Elle's big, handsome basketball player Zave sat holding her hand; she'd never looked more beautiful. Holly glowed as she stood near the tree next to her long-time love Elam, whose arm was draped over her shoulders. For the first time in years, Christmas felt like Christmas again, and I felt whole.

A bell jingled—Mom's Christmas bell. I could swear I heard her whisper, "Wedding bells." I swiped at a tear and grinned, thinking of my dear mother and how happy this scene would have made her—*perhaps she's here. No. Not perhaps. Mom and Dad are most definitely here.*

Charlie yelled, "Puppy!" and the rest of the kids squealed in delight. They immediately surrounded the little guy, who wiggled uncontrollably in response to all the attention.

The aroma of sizzling bacon filled my nose, and my mouth watered. Sweet nostalgia encircled me. Christmas warmth had returned to my heart, which no longer ached. We waded through shreds of wrapping paper strewn about. Obviously, the boys had already ripped into their presents.

Decker pulled the gifts from my bag and placed them next to the unopened packages, and I put a large envelope beside the gifts. I'd never seen a Christmas tree so beautiful. We found space on the loveseat and scooched close…to make room for Melba, of course. I couldn't remember feeling so happy.

"What's this, Chrissy?" Elle picked up the envelope.

"Get Holly and Joy and you can open it." I tried to act nonchalant when I felt anything but.

Everyone gathered to watch Noelle. She slit open the top and removed a legal document, then clapped a hand over her mouth. The others moved in for a closer look.

"The freeze on the Frost Foundation has been lifted?" Joy nearly yelped.

I cleared my throat and clutched Decker's hand. "Turns out, Elle," I directed my gaze to her, "you were right to suspect Uncle Simon; he was after Dad's inheritance." I took a long shuddering breath before I continued. "The even worse news is, we need a new lawyer." Now all eyes were on me. I explained how Simon and his partner had schemed together to freeze the account. "I happened upon them lunching at the Broadmoor, which was fortunate. There they'd worked through details to finish the deed—syphon the frozen assets and disappear."

Gasps rippled through the room.

"Luckily, they confessed all. It just took some persuasion—"

"And threat of an extended prison sentence," Decker added.

"Simon even had the audacity to inform me that he was far more entitled to his father's money than we are. After all, we each have successful careers." I swallowed some of the hateful emotion rising in my throat and took another breath. "I think he had gambling debts, or something. I'll admit it broke my heart."

"But you said we need a new lawyer." Elle tilted her head, confused.

I nodded. "It hurt to have our own flesh and blood do something so deceitful, but the real pain came when I realized his partner in all this was someone we know even better and trust—well, once trusted—Richard Arnett."

Stunned silence.

I knew it would be a tough pill to swallow. Betrayal hurt.

"Richard Arnett and Uncle Simon were working together?" Holly looked stricken—as did the others.

"That wasn't only our funds they were making off with; a lot of it had been donated," Elle said. "Not to mention, Simon had already inherited a mountain of money."

Joy shook her head, getting paler by the minute. "It explains why Mom and Dad never talked about Simon. I figured he and Dad didn't get along. Now, I'm thinking there must have been much more to it. But Richard…"

I nodded, wondering if Christmas really was the best time to share the news.

Finally, Joy lifted a glass of orange juice. "Well, I say Merry Christmas to us, and all the children who will benefit from the pediatric center."

"Hear, hear!" the rest of the group chimed in.

I released a breath. I hadn't known how they'd take it. Me, their little sister, managing important matters that concerned us all.

Decker squeezed my hand and kissed the top of my head.

Soon the room was abuzz again with happy chatter.

One by one, my sisters approached me to say how impressed they were with the way I'd handled the situation. My heart swelled. I thought it safe to say I'd grown up a bit this year.

When they'd all turned their attention back to individual conversations, Melba tapped me on the shoulder. "Nobody's in the kitchen just now." She winked, and her lips curved into a sly grin.

Decker gave me a puzzled look.

"C'mon. I've got something for you." We slipped into the kitchen where I pulled a slender box from my purse. "Here's your present."

His eyes widened. After removing the paper, he lifted the lid from the box and peered down at a golden keychain with "Dallas—Just a whisper away" and a heart engraved on it. He looked at me with watery eyes.

"I thought you'd want to have your brother near you. I hope it's not too—"

"It's perfect." He pulled me into his arms. "Thank you."

****

Merry Christmas, Chrissy. I know this day is difficult for you, but lately you've seemed like a new person—happy. I hope the upcoming new year will be a great one for you.

Love, Kassi

I read my roommate's Christmas card over and over, expecting her handwriting—so like my mother's—to cause at least a tremor in my heart—nope, not even a stutter. I'd never forget my parents, nor would I stop missing them, but now I knew I could move on with my life and not only find happiness but spread it as well.

Epilogue

Three Years Later

We all admired the Christmas gift Sean had presented to Joy this morning—a panoramic photo of the Nicholas Charles Frost Pediatric Center. Completed two years ago, it looked as if it had been part of Memorial Hospital all along. Zave and Sean fastened the art above the fireplace—a spot seemingly held in reserve for that very picture.

"It's beautiful," I whispered.

Decker nodded. "It is. And you girls should be proud of what you accomplished. But right now, I think you'd better give your attention to the princess of the family, before she sends you to the dungeon."

The men quickly joined the fun, while Charlie and the twins began to cheer.

"Ahem." Eight-year-old Tatum placed fisted hands on her petite hips and stood near the Christmas tree. She waited until she had everyone's attention, including mine. "Remember, don't let them go until I clap my hands."

I pinched my lips together to suppress a laugh. After all, Tatum had made it crystal-clear that toddler-racing was serious business.

She pointed to a star-shaped Christmas cookie on the coffee table. "The baby who crosses the magic sparkle finish line first gets that."

The babies were looking everywhere but at the tinsel Tatum had strewn out to form a line.

"On your mark. Get set. Go!" She clapped and we all set our toddlers loose.

Decker and I cheered hard for our own chunky cherub, but he didn't stand a chance against Elle's little guy. No, that one rose an inch or two above the rest, clearly taking after his basketball-playing father. Holly and Elam's baby sat down in the middle of the race, tripping up the rest, but somehow Joy's baby reached the…uh oh.

"No, Nicky-boy. You can't have the cookie. You gotta cross the magic sparkle line." Tatum stomped her foot. "Nicholas Sean Summers, drop that cookie!"

Too late. Baby Nicky had the baked good in his mouth before anyone could stop him.

He turned to Tatum, red frosting covering his fingers and pudgy cheeks, and gave her the most innocent look.

The room erupted in laughter—from everyone but cute little Tatum, that was. She was busy glaring at the cookie monster.

We Frost girls had delivered four healthy boys around a year ago—give or take a week—a new generation of Frost Christmas babies to love. I thought our parents were up there happily arranging things for us in their crazy, cheesy, oh-so-loveable way… Or, maybe March was just a very cozy month.

In case you missed the beginning of this series, you'll want to start with the first book…

Finding Joy

by

Joyce Horstmann

Here's how it begins:

Chapter One

"This is clearly a case of adult peer pressure gone wild," I mumbled as I hung up the phone. "Am I really that pathetically lonely?"

All three of my younger sisters had called me to insist for the hundredth time that I needed to stop dragging my heels and go to the support-group meeting that weekend.

"Just try it," said Elle.

"You will meet people who know how you feel," urged Holly.

And, "You need to get out of the house and talk to adults," added Chrissy. They had all offered to babysit my boys as well, which left me no excuse, unfortunately.

I finished loading the dishwasher and heard the loud *ping* of the timer on the dryer. As I pulled out a load of little boys' clothes and started folding the denim jeans and superhero t-shirts, I thought about Tom for at least the tenth time that morning; how I wished he were here to see his sons growing up and changing so much.

The twins, Micah and Mitchell, were babies when their father went back to the Middle East for his third— and last—deployment. Their big brother, Charlie, was only five, and his memories had slowly become mixed in with the stories I told him. "Daddy's in heaven," he said sadly before bedtime prayers.

Yes, little man, your daddy's in heaven. So far away.

I'd agreed to go to that meeting, the Colorado Springs Chapter of the Widows and Widowers Support Group, against my better judgment. It sounded dreadful. I didn't want to hang out with a bunch of sad people and listen to their depressing stories. I knew all about loneliness and mourning. I was living it every day.

Piling the folded clothes into the big, red laundry basket, I pricked up my ears to determine if I could hear any sounds of torture or rioting coming from the boys' rooms. Nothing. I sighed in relief, even though I knew this could also mean trouble. *Peace rules for now.* Then I heard giggling, followed by a loud thump. Well, I knew it couldn't last.

As I tried to picture the members of the social gathering coming up in a few days, I imagined I'd find myself surrounded by about fifty widows and a couple of sixty-something-year-old widowers. "Fun times," I said to myself.

I looked over at a picture of Tom on the mantel, standing jauntily on a ski slope at Aspen, the beautiful snow-covered Rockies behind him. His dark-brown eyes and handsome smile radiated out, filling the room with love and happiness. I missed him so much. The loneliness could be overwhelming, and that was why my sisters had urged me to form new friendships with people who understood the heaviness of grief.

I heard more giggles coming from Charlie's room, including a squeal of delight from Micah—who could easily call pigs to the barn with that piercing voice— and I smiled in gratitude for the three of them. Tom's boys. Tom's legacy.

I'd had a lot of grief during my life. More than my share, I think. My baby brother passed away from heart disease when I was just a kid, and my mother and father died in a car accident on the day after Christmas four years ago, which had ruined the holidays for us sisters ever since. Our lives changed in an instant—one terrible moment in time. A drunk driver killed them. He walked away unscathed.

The month of December used to be the most wonderful time of the year. Mom and Dad had evidently been kind of crazy in their first years of marriage: they planned five December babies and hit the jackpot every time. Well, almost every time. Little Nicholas arrived three weeks early, on November thirtieth. He still received a "holiday" name, though. I'm Joy, and I was born on Christmas Eve. Just short of three years later came Noelle, who goes by Elle;

followed two years later, almost to the day, by Holly; and our baby sister, Christina Marie, arrived five years less six days later. "A Holiday Quartet," my dad used to say. The tail-ender of the family, Nicky, joined us nearly four years later. To add one more punch line to the whole Christmastime cuteness, our last name is Frost. It would only be more outrageous if our parents were Mr. and Mrs. Jack.

A word about the author...

Jeanie Davis and her husband, Rick, live in Gilbert, Arizona. She loves peach ice cream, shopping, a clean house...oh, and chocolate, of course. She has traveled extensively—from Fiji to Africa and Europe to Costa Rica—but prefers being at home creating new adventures on her computer.

Her four daughters have left her nest empty, but they return often with grandchildren who bring the real fun and adventure to her life.

A good romance will always capture Jeanie's attention; add suspense or historical ties and she's totally hooked. She's the author of an historical fiction novel, *As Ever Yours*, based on the lives of her grandparents, a children's Christmas book, *I Don't Know Why I Did It*, and two romantic suspense novels, *Time Twist* and *Time Trap*, books one and two of the Somerset series. Book three, *Time Torn*, is coming soon.

She is passionate about writing and always has a new story to delve into or an older one to revise. She began by writing poetry and music, which she still enjoys.

When she's not spoiling her grandchildren, Jeanie spends her free time curled up with a good book or typing away on her most recent mystery, adventure, or romance.

CPSIA information can be obtained
at www.ICGtesting.com
Printed in the USA
BVHW090906281220
596438BV00010B/674